"Do you think a m **and power, having what I went throu** **be willing to stand idly by while my child is shuffled between minders, airplanes, movie locations and court-mandated visitation rights?"**

Goldie's mouth trembled for a second before she caught ahold of it. "Gael—"

He broke off midpace and planted himself firmly in front of her. He needed her to see the intent emblazoned in his heart and mind. "Let me answer for you, Goldie. The scenario you propose will happen *over my dead body.*"

"You can't just rule things out, Gael. We need to agree to a compromise."

"Why compromise when I have a solution?" he said.

Her smooth forehead wrinkled in a frown. "We confirmed the pregnancy less than ten minutes ago. How can you have a solution already?"

"Very easily, when the situation is this important."

She gave a slight shake of her head, but her gaze didn't leave his. She blinked, her expression turning trepidatious. "No. I think we need to talk about this some more."

"I'm done talking, Goldie. The soundest solution to the situation we find ourselves in is for you to marry me."

Rival Brothers

When rivalry is thicker than blood...

Estranged brothers Alejandro and Gael Aguilar
are titans of technology and
each other's biggest rivals.

It will take two special women to help these
sexy Spaniards put the past behind them
and join forces to become more powerful
than they ever dreamed!

Battle commences in

A Deal with Alejandro

And find out who will be victorious in

One Night with Gael

Maya Blake

ONE NIGHT WITH GAEL

Recycling programs
for this product may
not exist in your area.

ISBN-13: 978-0-373-13483-0

One Night with Gael

First North American Publication 2016

Copyright © 2016 by Maya Blake

This edition published by arrangement with Harlequin Books S.A.

For questions and comments about the quality of this book, please contact us at CustomerService@Harlequin.com.

Printed in U.S.A.

Maya Blake's hopes of becoming a writer were born when she picked up her first romance at thirteen. Little did she know her dream would come true! Does she still pinch herself every now and then to make sure it's not a dream? Yes, she does! Feel free to pinch her, too, via Twitter, Facebook or Goodreads! Happy reading!

Books by Maya Blake

Harlequin Presents

Signed Over to Santino
A Diamond Deal with the Greek
A Marriage Fit for a Sinner
Married for the Prince's Convenience
Innocent in His Diamonds
His Ultimate Prize
Marriage Made of Secrets
The Sinful Art of Revenge
The Price of Success

Rival Brothers

A Deal with Alejandro

The Billionaire's Legacy

The Di Sione Secret Baby

Secret Heirs of Billionaires

Brunetti's Secret Son

The Untameable Greeks

What the Greek's Money Can't Buy
What the Greek Can't Resist
What the Greek Wants Most

The 21st Century Gentleman's Club

The Ultimate Playboy

Visit the Author Profile page at Harlequin.com for more titles.

For Romy, for your invaluable help with all things South Africa. Any mistakes are mine!

CHAPTER ONE

POR EL AMOR de todo lo que es santo! For the love of everything that's holy!

Gael Aguilar gritted his teeth and stopped short of invoking actual martyred saints as he listened to excuse after excuse roll off the tongue of the man he was talking to on the phone.

At the end of his very short tether, he cut across yet another effusive apology. 'Let me get this straight. You're supposed to be here, in New York, holding auditions, but instead you chose to go skiing, in *Switzerland*, and are now laid up in hospital?'

'It was just supposed to be a weekend thing for my wife's birthday, but… Look, believe me, no one's more sorry than I am, okay?'

Not okay. Gael jerked his head back against the car's headrest none-too-gently. 'What's the medical verdict?'

'Leg's broken in two places. It's going in a cast tomorrow. Provided there are no further complications I'll be back in New York on Thursday, to pick things up, but we can't miss the Othello Arts Institute slot today. It's been arranged for months.'

Ethan Ryland, his director, was almost pleading. Gael barely stopped himself from pointing out that he should have known better then than to indulge himself with a continental trip. He also barely stopped himself from uttering the pithy words that would have brought him immense satisfaction right then and there. But temporary relief wouldn't alter the facts facing him.

He couldn't fire the director. Somewhere in the small print of his multipage contract was the perfect excuse for what was happening now, Gael was sure. Had he not had bigger matters demanding his attention, he would have taken the time to seek out other small print, words that swung in his favour, and used them. Hell, he wouldn't even need to lift a finger himself. That was, after all, why his company had a whole firm of lawyers on retainer.

But he couldn't do that. For one thing, embroiling the Atlas Group, the staggeringly successful but still infant global conglomerate he'd birthed with his half-brother in litigation right now would be bad for business. Not only would his half-brother Alejandro take satisfaction in demanding his head on a platter, their Japanese partners the Ishikawa brothers would also have a thing or two to say about the matter.

The merger between their three companies was barely six months old—as was his personal relationship with Alejandro, following decades of their actively and conspicuously avoiding each other.

While the business side of their relationship had flourished after a few initial setbacks, personal interaction between him and his brother had taken a two-steps-forward-one-step-back approach. Their once-a-month business meetings had grown decidedly stilted in the past three months and, frankly, Gael was on the verge of deciding it was time to take a permanent step back and run his side of the business from his Silicon Valley base.

It didn't matter that he knew the reason why.

The past. Always the past. And not just *his*. His mother's. His father's—the father who'd been woefully lacking in being worthy of the name. Alejandro himself.

He pushed the recent confrontation with his mother aside, stepped back from the thoughts of torrid retribution he harboured towards his director, and forced himself to speak. 'What exactly do you wish me to do?' he snarled.

'Just sit in on a cast call. You know my work—that's why you hired me. You also know what you want. It will be filmed, of course, so I'll see it when I get back. But nothing beats experiencing the raw, visceral performance in person. Tapping in to the emotions of acting is only potent on camera if it's saturating in real life.'

Gael exhaled and curbed the urge to roll his eyes at the melodrama of the director's speech. 'Send me the details. I will attend this meeting you've set up,' he snapped into the silence thickening in the back of his limo.

A breath of relief shot from the sleek phone console at Gael's elbow. 'Thanks, Gael. I owe you one.'

'You owe me more than one. You owe me a first-class Atlas Studios maiden movie, to be unveiled—hiccup-free—as part of my digital streaming relaunch in six months' time. Make no mistake: you only get this one free pass. Let me down again and you'll be out. Is that clear?'

'Crystal.'

Gael hung up before more useless platitudes reached his ears and instructed his driver to alter their destination. It looked as if he was staying in New York for one more night.

Activating the phone again, he dialled a familiar number in Chicago. As he waited for his brother to pick up Gael admitted to himself that he felt the tiniest sliver of relief to have avoided the Chicago trip for one more day. Because, contrary to the challenge he'd thrown down to Alejandro a year ago, about his brother acknowledging him as his blood, Gael himself had never been inclined to claim the Aguilar name. No matter that there wasn't any doubt as to his parentage, the name had never sat well on his shoulders.

After all, he was a bastard whose mother had tried to cloak his name in imagined respectability by naming him after the father who hadn't wanted him. Had his mother not pleaded with him, Gael would've changed his surname to Vega years ago. But she'd beseeched him—out of the same bewildering devotion to the man she'd chosen to reproduce with, he was sure. And he'd relented. He'd withstood both the blatant and the silent mockery from strangers and gossipmongers from childhood into adulthood for as long as he could. Then, like his half-brother, he'd retreated to the other side of the world.

The news that their father was once again indulging in the extramarital affairs that had brought Gael into the world had turned his stomach. Alejandro, for his part, after a series of conversations with his parents, seemed a lot less bitter about the whole thing. Not so much Gael.

And, on top of that stomach-turning news, his last conversation with his mother hadn't ended well when he'd found out *she* was entertaining his father's advances again. Nor had the exchange he'd had with Alejandro lent any insight into why their respective biological parents were hell-bent on perpetuating chaos.

'Do I want to know what you're thinking?'

Alejandro's question, posed after one too many whiskies in his brother's office a few short weeks ago, slashed into Gael's brain.

'No.'

His brother's brooding gaze settled on him. 'Tell me anyway.'

'I'm wondering why polygamy was ever banned,' Gael had responded.

Low, bitter laughter had spilled from his half-brother. 'Trust me, I'm a one-woman man, but the same thought has crossed my mind many times about our parents.'

'You know what? I don't think they'd be happy with polygamy, even were it an option. They'd still find a way to make their lives—and ours—a living hell.'

Sour amusement had disappeared under the cloud that always accompanied thoughts of his father and mother.

He didn't like to lump them together as *his parents* because they'd never been that to him. Sure, Tomas Aguilar had attempted to make a mockery of a family with his mother when Gael was a child, but that had been more to do with his twisted game to hurt the wife who had worn his ring and borne his firstborn than with love for Gael or his mother.

His father, his mother…his past…had nothing to do with the issue that confronted him now. And he'd never been one to expend energy on fruitless ventures.

Gael arrived on the doorstep of the Othello Arts Institute late—courtesy of an accident on the Queensborough Bridge—and alighted from the back of the limo in a fouler mood than he'd been in two hours before.

Not because of the call with his director, or even the chaotic traffic. No, his teeth-grinding could be laid firmly at his brother's feet.

Alejandro had been nauseatingly understanding of Gael's excuses, even going as far as to put Elise, his fiancée, on the line, to reassure Gael that all was well and they would welcome him to Chicago any time he pleased.

Wondering whether his brother's brooding tone had been meant to reassure him, or to deliver a subtle message that Alejandro still maintained an arm's-length approach to their relationship, despite Gael himself wishing it so, was what had thrown him into a worse mood.

He pushed open the glass doors to the sharp-angled building and entered the world-renowned institution, clearly aware he was spoiling for a fight. He didn't bother taking a steadying breath because it would be of no use. Only two methods restored his control when he felt like this—losing himself in computer code or losing himself between the thighs of a woman. One had made him richer than his wildest dreams. The other never failed to restore equilibrium to his very male aggression.

The urge to pull out his phone and arrange his next assignation with his flavour of the month was only curbed by the reminder that this inconvenient detour was still business. And business *always*—without exception—came before pleasure.

He sought directions to the room he needed and entered to find two casting directors ready and waiting.

An hour later Gael's mood had taken a sharp dip further south. The auditions had gone worse than abysmally—and he'd arrived from the viewpoint of an outsider. Tense handshakes with the directors and a swift exit preceded his urge to go back on his word and fire his director immediately. If this was what he had in store then he was better off parting company with Ethan Ryland before the process advanced beyond salvaging.

Sí, someone most definitely needed to atone for his mood. He pulled the phone from his pocket.

And stopped.

The door to his left was only partially ajar, but he heard her clearly. Her voice, filled with pure, unadulterated emotion, carried even without being raised high.

Removing his hovering thumb from the call button, he pushed the door with his forefinger. When it started to creak he stopped and stepped back. Glancing up and down the quiet hallway, Gael saw another door farther away at the end of the auditorium. Quick strides granted him silent entry into the shadowed rear of the cavernous room in time to catch her impassioned speech.

'You won't leave me. I won't let you. You think you love her, but you don't. And, yes, I know you enough to tell you what is in your heart. I love you that much, Simon. Enough to forgive. Enough to take another chance on us. But for us to happen you need to stay. Please...take the chance.'

Gael realised he was holding his breath as he watched tears stream down her face. She raged for another minute, then collapsed onto the stage. Genuine sobs convulsed her petite body.

Against his will, he was riveted, the breath he'd scoffed at needing moments ago locked in his throat. He watched her struggle to her feet, saw a hiccup shake through her as the last of her emotion rippled free. She swiped at the tears with her wrists and walked to the edge of the stage, chest rising and falling, her gaze expectantly on the audition director—who stared at her for uncomfortably tense seconds without speaking.

A fizzle of irritation wove through Gael's body and his already black mood darkened further at the director's deliberate silence.

'Your performance was...commendable, Miss Beckett. I can tell you poured your heart into it.'

A tiny hopeful smile from the performer. 'Thank you. I did.' The response was firm, but husky, probably owing to her emotional expenditure.

The director regretfully shook his head. 'But sadly I need more than that. Heart is great, but what I need is *soul.*'

The actress frowned. 'I don't understand. That *was* my heart—*and* my soul.'

'In your opinion. But not in mine.'

Gael felt her acute disappointment from across the room. She gave a slight shake of her head, as if to refute the director's words. Then she gathered herself with admirable pride. 'I'm sorry you think so. But thank you for your time.'

She started across the stage towards a shabby-looking rucksack near the door.

'That's it?'

The smirking taunt from the director tightened the knot of anger in Gael's gut.

She paused. 'Excuse me?'

'According to your opening speech, you want this part more than you want your next meal. And yet you're walking away without so much as a fight?' the director sneered.

Her eyes widened. 'I thought you said… You mean I have a chance?'

'Everyone has a chance, Miss Beckett. What stands between you and the opportunities you receive, however, is how much you *want* it. Are you prepared to do whatever it takes?'

She nodded immediately. 'Yes, I am.'

The director crooked his finger. She retraced her steps to the middle of the stage. Impatiently he beckoned her further forward. She approached without hesitation.

The beginnings of distaste filled Gael's mouth as he watched naked hunger fill her face.

Somewhere in the middle of her performance she'd lost her shoes. Her bare toes breached the edge of the hardwood stage as she looked down at the director. He extracted a silver card from his pocket, traced it over the top of one foot down to her toes before laying it between her slightly parted feet.

'*This* is what it'll take, Miss Beckett. Pick it up and the part is yours.'

Gael had been on the receiving end of propositions for long enough to know what was going on. *Dios mio*, hadn't he had the row of all rows with his mother only two weeks ago over just such an issue?

He expelled his breath in a quietly seething rush as he watched her slowly sink down and retrieve what looked unmistakably like a hotel room key card.

The disappointment that lanced through him was strong enough to make him question why the scene unfolding in front of him was affecting him so deeply. Perhaps today of all days, when the past seemed to be dogging him with its bitter memories, he'd wanted to be pleasantly surprised by the elusive integrity of the human spirit. To experience a pure character to go along with the pure performance that had stopped him in his tracks, touched him in ways he was still grappling with.

More fool him.

As the director's hands moved to touch her feet Gael retreated as silently as he'd entered, his rigid gaze firmly averted from the sleazy scene unfolding on the stage.

He was looking for a fairy tale where none existed. Just as he'd once—futilely and childishly—prayed for a family that included a father who didn't wish him out of existence.

He should know better. No. He *had* known better—for a very long time.

Even before he exited the building he knew those dredged-up feelings would be crushed beneath the immovable titanium power of his ambition and success. Emotional needs and futile dreams were far behind him. What he'd done with his life since that time in Spain was what mattered.

Everything else came a very pale second.

CHAPTER TWO

So why was he back here mere hours later, pulling up in front of Othello? And at a time of night when there was guaranteed to be no one around?

Gael had resisted admitting it all day. But, despite the stomach-turning denouement, something about the woman's performance itself had stayed with him. Enough to make him pass a few precious hours re-reading the carefully selected script he'd searched through thousands for before settling on two years ago. Enough to convince him to put aside his personal feelings and revisit the actress's flawless performance.

And it *had* been flawless. With a true visionary's direction she would be able to pull off the project he had in mind for his movie launch without a hitch. Help him achieve the best possible premiere for what would be the world's largest independent streaming entity.

The project wasn't by any means the only thing sustaining the launch, but if done right the results and the benefit to the whole conglomerate would be incomparable. His partners were counting on him to get this right. *He* was counting on himself to make this vision come true.

That was why he was here, approaching the front desk with little more than a surname and a firm grip on his distaste.

The receptionist looked up, did a double take that would have amused him had his mood been anything but grim.

'Uh…may I help you, sir?' she asked eagerly.

'You have a student—a Miss Beckett. She was performing in room 307 this afternoon. I'd like to speak to her, *por favor.*'

The enthusiasm dimmed a touch. 'Do you have her first name?'

Gael frowned. 'No.'

The receptionist grimaced. 'I'm sorry, sir, I can't locate her without a first name.'

'You have a lot of students named Beckett?' he enquired.

'I can't give out that information, or even tell you if she's a student here or not. The thing is, she may not be. We hold outside auditions here from time to time. She may have come in with a director…' She stopped and cast a slightly uncomfortable glance at him, probably due to his increasing irritation with her babbling. 'Sorry, sir, but if you want to leave a card…or your contact details… I'll see what I can do?'

The smile was re-emerging, and the flick of her hair was transmitting signals he didn't want to acknowledge.

With reluctance, Gael extracted his card and handed

it over. She glanced at it, her eyes going wider still as she gave a soft gasp. He watched, his cynicism growing, as realisation and an accompanying degree of avarice entered her eyes.

His former company, Toredo Inc., had been a serious player on the streaming media platform—a hit with students and young professionals long before he'd teamed up with Alejandro and the Ishikawa brothers to form Atlas. Since then, he and his partners had rarely left the media's attention.

He and Alejandro had only finished their world tour scouting to find satellite partners to enter into a joint venture with Atlas a few short months ago. During that time they'd conducted numerous media interviews, which meant his face had been plastered all over the news for weeks on end. Anyone with a decent search engine knew what the Aguilar brothers looked like, and how much they were worth—and, if their search had been thorough enough, their relationship status.

From her expression, the receptionist was no exception. He watched her cast an amusingly exaggerated look round the deserted reception area before clicking on the keyboard in front of her.

'I think you're looking for Goldie Beckett?' she stage-whispered.

The name brought to mind corkscrew golden curls and honey-toned skin. Surprisingly fitting. *'Sí,'* he confirmed. The chances of the name being wrong were minimal. If it was, he could always resume the search.

The receptionist nodded. 'I really shouldn't be doing

this…but she was practising in the music room until five minutes ago. You just missed her.'

Gael stifled a curse. 'Did you see which way she went?'

'No, but I know she lives in Jersey, so she may be headed for the subway?'

'Thank you,' he bit out.

'Uh…you're welcome…'

She looked as if she wanted to continue the conversation. But Gael turned away, cutting short the familiar look that preceded a gentle but firm demand for something. A phone number. A favour for a friend. A *personal* favour. At any other time he would have been inclined to grant the mousy receptionist another minute of his time, even reward her for her help. He'd long accepted how things worked between him and the opposite sex. He gave when the mood took him. They took *all* the time—until he called a halt to their schemes and often naked greed.

But not tonight.

Not when an alien urgency rubbed under his skin, demanding he find the elusive Miss Goldie Beckett.

He rushed out into the street, already condemning the futility of his actions. This was New York City. Finding a single person in a throng of people on the sidewalk, even after nine at night, was insane. And yet his feet moved inexorably in the direction of the subway station. Behind him his chauffeur kept pace in the limo. Probably he was wondering what had possessed his employer, Gael mused.

He knew her name. All he had to do was pass it to

his security people and let them find her. He'd witnessed her naked ambition for himself. All he needed to do to entice her was offer his name and the once-in-a-lifetime project he had in mind and she would come running. There was absolutely no need for him to pound the pavement.

He'd slowed his footsteps, thinking how idiotic he looked when he heard a scuffle in the alleyway.

Gael almost walked past. Unsavoury characters lurking in dark places were commonplace in cities such as this.

A husky cry and the flash of golden curls caught the corner of his eye. He stopped in his tracks, wondering if he was conjuring her up in his irritated desperation.

The alley was poorly lit, but not deep. His eyes narrowed as he tried to peer through the wisps of smoke pouring out of a nearby restaurant vent.

'No, damn you, let go!'

The distinctive voice coupled with the decisive sound of clothing being ripped firmly altered his course, hurrying him towards the night-shrouded scene.

'Lady, I won't say it again. Give me the bag.' A low, menacing voice sounded through the gloom.

A bold, mocking laugh. 'At least you have the good manners to call me *lady* as you attempt to steal my property.'

'It'll be more than an attempt in a second if you don't let go of the damn bag!'

The warning was followed by more sounds of a tussle. Then a muted scream, the distinctive thud of a body landing heavily and a hiss of pain.

Gael arrived at the scene in time to see a dark shadow loom at him, then rush past. The blocking move he threw out missed by a whisker, and the assailant was already rushing out of the alley. He had a split second to debate whether to go after the mugger or aid the victim. Gael chose the latter.

The vision before him scrambled upright from the grimy concrete. 'God, no! Stop him! He's got my purse!'

This time he caught the bundle that attempted to launch past him. Arms flailed in his hold. A firm, sinewy body twisted in his arms as he held her tight.

'Dammit, let me go. He's got my belongings.'

'Calm yourself. You won't catch him. He's long gone by now,' he replied, attempting to keep hold of the wriggling creature.

'Only because you're letting him get away. For God's sake, let me go.' She stopped suddenly. 'Hell, you're his accomplice, aren't you?' she accused.

Gael reeled back in amused shock. '*Perdón?* You think I'm a *thief*?'

'I don't know what the heck you are. All I know is you're stopping me from going after that piece of scum who's just stolen my purse. What am I supposed to think?'

She pulled at his hold. Gael thought it was probably wise to let her go, but his hands wouldn't co-operate.

'You're supposed to thank a person who has just come to your aid,' he suggested.

Eyes of an indeterminate colour widened in disbelief. 'He got my stuff *before* you arrived. You let him get away—and you think I should be *grateful*?' she spat with quiet fury.

She had fire—he granted her that. But it was the shaking in her voice that drew his attention.

Gael gripped her arms in a firmer hold, careful not to spook her further. Although he was still mildly amused she thought him a thief, her agitation meant she might take flight if he let her go. 'I'm not a thief, Miss Beckett. I assure you.'

She froze. And in the darkness he was beginning to become acclimatised to her gaze searched his with growing suspicion.

'How do you know my name?' she demanded, her voice husky with a different kind of emotion.

Fear.

That didn't sit well with him. He let her go and stepped back, although he made sure to keep himself between her and the exit. Now he had her before him he wasn't in the mood to go searching for her again should she bolt.

'You have nothing to fear from me.'

She laughed mockingly, but her trepidation didn't abate. 'Says the man who's keeping from leaving. Don't think I didn't notice the body-block. I'm warning you—I know Krav Maga.'

Again a tendril of amusement twitched at a corner of his lips. 'So do I, *pequeña*. Perhaps we can spar some other time, when we're both in the mood.'

'I don't spar just for the fun of it. I fight to defend myself. Now, either tell me why you're here wasting my time, and how you know my name, or get out of my way.'

'Your assailant is long gone. If you wish to report the incident I'm willing to lend you my phone.'

'No, thanks. If you want to do something useful will yourself into getting out of my way instead, why don't you?'

Gael shook his head. 'Not until we've talked.'

'I don't know who you are or what you could possibly have to talk to me about that involves us standing in a dark, smelly alley.'

She started to skirt him. He let her go until she faced the exit and her perceived freedom.

'I'm here because you're of interest to me.'

'I highly doubt that.' She took a few steps backwards. Stumbled. Her breath caught as she righted herself. 'I don't know what your problem is, but I assure you I'm not worth stalking, if that's your thing. And the sum total of my worth—which was eighty dollars—is now headed for the other side of the city, thanks to you. Anything else you want won't be given willingly.'

She retreated a couple more steps, until she stood beneath the single lit bulb gracing the mouth of the alley.

Gael inhaled sharply. He'd thought her performance captivating across the wide expanse of an auditorium. At the time he hadn't paid much attention to the woman herself. But he was looking now. And up close Goldie Beckett was…something else. Her dark honey-toned skin, even under the poor lighting, was vibrant and silky-smooth, her high cheekbones, velvety pouting lips and determined chin, a perfect enough combination to make his breath snag somewhere in his chest.

He wasn't by any means new to the art of appreciating beautiful women. His electronic contact lists were filled with more than his fair share of phone numbers from past and possible future conquests. But there was something uniquely enthralling about Goldie Beckett's face that riveted his attention.

Perhaps it was her eyes. Gael wasn't sure whether they were blue, or the violet he suspected, but the big, alluring pools, even though they currently glared at him, were nevertheless absorbing enough to keep him staring.

As for her body... She couldn't be more than five foot five, but even her lack of height—he preferred his women taller—didn't detract from her attraction. Nor did it diminish the curvy frame currently wrapped in a black sweater and denim skirt in any way.

A *torn* black sweater, which gaped wide enough at the shoulder to reveal the strap of a lilac-coloured bra and the top of one voluptuous breast.

A thick silence ensued, during which she noticed where his gaze had landed. He admonished himself to get control in the few seconds before her hand snapped up to cover herself.

Her glare intensified even as her other hand crept around her neck and patted in a puzzled search. 'Oh, great!' she muttered eventually.

'Something wrong?' Gael asked, forcing his gaze from the hand covering her breast.

'Don't you mean something *else* wrong?' she snapped. 'Yes, something else *is* wrong. That...that lowlife didn't just take my purse, he took my scarf too.'

Again there was a thin tremble in her voice that struck him the wrong way.

She was probably no longer apprehensive of his presence, but she'd been attacked and robbed. A closer scrutiny of her showed another rip in her tights and muddy scuff marks on her skirt and boots.

'Are you hurt?'

Her mouth pursed and her eyes darkened. She regarded him, debating whether to furnish him with an answer. Slowly her free hand opened to reveal a bloodied deep welt across her palm.

A quiet fury rolled to life in his belly.

He balled his fist in his pocket to stop himself from reaching out to examine the wound more closely. He was absolutely sure she wouldn't welcome the move. 'My car is parked over there.' He indicated with a jerk of chin. 'If you come with me I'll get you cleaned up. Before we talk.'

Her laughter mocked again, deeper this time. 'I'm from New Jersey, Mr...whatever your name is, not Narnia. I don't step through cupboards or into limos, however flash they look, out of naive curiosity.'

Gael gritted his teeth, reached into his pocket and brought out his business card. 'My name is Gael Aguilar. I'm working on a project I think you might be interested in. I saw your...performance this afternoon and came back to look for you. The receptionist mentioned you'd just left. I came in this direction in the hope of finding you. Need I go on?'

She eyed him warily. 'You hesitated before you said *"performance"*. Why?'

Gael was a little surprised that she hadn't immediately jumped at the mention of his name, and that she wasn't preening at the thought of being pursued as he'd pursued her. Most women would find that a compliment. But what shocked him more was that she'd cut through everything he'd said and singled out the slight trip in his voice triggered by what he'd witnessed after her audition that afternoon.

It wasn't a flaw he wanted to dwell on. This wasn't personal. It was business.

The reminder, and the fact that he'd been in this alley too long, tautened his voice. 'It's not productive to dwell on the cadence of my speech, Miss Beckett. You have my word that I mean you no harm.' His gaze dropped to her hand. 'My advice, though, would be to see to that wound before it gets infected. I can help. Then we can talk. I don't want anything more from you.'

A slight frown marred her forehead before she looked over his shoulder at the limo. His driver stood to attention next to the back door and inclined his head at her. Her frown cleared.

Pressing home the advantage the sight his burly bodyguard and driver provided, Gael continued. 'Unless I'm mistaken, you now have no means of reaching your destination tonight or contacting anyone for help?'

'I'm far from as helpless are you're making me sound, Mr Aguilar,' she muttered, although her voice lacked conviction.

He remained silent, gave her time to arrive at the conclusion he needed. After a minute she held out her hand.

He handed her his card and she stared down at it. If she recognised the information there she gave no indication. She looked from him to the car, then at the card, and back to him.

'You have a first aid kit in your car?' she enquired, quietly but firmly.

He probably did, but he shrugged. 'Possibly. I've never had occasion to use one. But my hotel is fifteen minutes away. We can get you cleaned up more efficiently there.'

She immediately shook her head. 'No, sorry— that won't work for me. That Narnia thing again, you know…?'

Gael stopped himself from growling his frustration. Never had he had to work this hard to get traction with a member of the opposite sex. Had he been in a better mood he would have been vastly amused. He shoved both hands into his pockets and thought fast.

'I was supposed to attend a dinner party tonight, with thirty other guests, on the Upper East Side. I pulled out because of the prospect of a business meeting with you. We will go there. Is that enough reassurance for you?'

She stared back at him, her injured fist slowly curling. Gael knew the abrasion would be causing her discomfort by now.

'Maybe…but how do I know the party is real and not some made-up fantasy?'

He compressed his lips before reaching for his phone. A few clicks and Pietro Vitale's face filled his screen.

'Gael, your presence has been missed. I've tried not to be insulted by a few of my female guests complaining that the party isn't the same without you,' his friend complained.

Gael's gaze shifted from the screen to Goldie. Her mouth was set in a firm, mildly disapproving line. He angled the screen towards her and addressed Pietro. 'I can remedy that, provided I can bring a guest?'

'Of course, *amico*. More is merrier, *si*? Also, the sooner, the better. *Arrivederci!*'

The Italian signed off.

'Will that suffice or do I need to request a police escort as well?' he drawled.

Goldie slowly shrugged. 'This is fine.'

Gael exhaled, a curious tension leaving his body as he nodded. 'Then come.'

Her eyes widened a fraction at his curt command, but she fell into step beside him. She summoned a tiny smile for his driver as he opened the back door for her. When she stooped to enter Gael forced his gaze from lingering on her rounded backside and shapely legs.

He entered after her and settled back in his seat. When she slid as far away from him as possible he experienced that mild irritation again. Considering what he'd witnessed in the auditorium this afternoon, her stand-offish behaviour was getting old.

'We've established that I'm not about to force myself on you, Miss Beckett, so perhaps you could drop the terrified lamb routine?'

'I'm not a lamb,' she snapped. 'And this isn't a routine.'

'Are you saying you're *always* this suspicious of everyone?'

'I'm suspicious of men who come out of nowhere

and accost me in dark alleys—and, yes, men who are possibly wolves dressed in lambs' clothing.'

'And yet here you are,' he said.

Her expressive eyes snapped at him. 'What exactly are you saying?'

Gael stared at her as the car slid into traffic. 'I mean your options aren't looking very good right now. So perhaps a little gratitude wouldn't go amiss. I might decide you're not worth the effort and leave you to your fate. Is that what you want?' he asked, watching her closely.

'I've just been attacked. I'm within my rights to be wary,' she replied.

'Yes, but I think you trust your instincts too—which is why you're here, *no*?'

'You think you know me?' she enquired, narrow-eyed.

'I think my assessment is right. Instinct first, then after that you let other…urges guide you.'

'What's that supposed to mean? What urges?'

His mouth twisted. 'You tell me.'

'I have no idea what you're talking about. And if this is the way our supposed business meeting is heading perhaps I'm better off cutting my losses right now.'

Gael sighed. 'While you decide on that will you allow me to put your seat belt on for you? I wouldn't want you to suffer another injury en route to what you imagine is your gruesome end.'

Her eyes narrowed. 'You're mocking me?'

He reached for the seat belt. 'I'm trying to find a way to have a conversation without getting disagreed with at every turn.'

She inhaled long and hard, her gaze going from the buckle in his hand to his face. When he cocked an eyebrow she nodded and pressed herself back against the seat. Moving closer, Gael wondered whether his offer had been a good idea. Underneath the distinctive smell of her intimate acquaintance with alley concrete he caught the scent of apples and honeysuckle. And at close quarters he saw her pulse racing at her throat, her skin flushing when he drew the belt between her breasts.

The stirring in his groin wasn't surprising—he was a red-blooded male, after all—but he cursed its presence all the same, especially when he cradled her hip for a precious few seconds before the lock slid home and his blood heated up to discomfort levels.

When he finished the task and sat back it wasn't without a modicum of relief.

He was almost glad when she cleared her throat. 'So, what do you want to talk to me about?'

He brought his mind firmly back to task. To business. 'I have a proposition for you. If you're agreeable we'll get you cleaned up first, then we'll talk, *si*?'

CHAPTER THREE

GOLDIE TRIED TO FOCUS as the sleek, luxurious car rolled down Columbus Avenue and turned on to Central Park West. She didn't think she'd hit her head when that horrid brute had wrestled her purse away from her. And yet a hazy sensation, as if she'd fallen down a rabbit hole, swirled all around her, making her wonder if her faculties were intact. Making her wonder if she'd heard him right.

What had this unfathomably riveting stranger said? A *proposition*.

She wanted to snort under her breath. Nothing good could come out of a proposition from a man like *that*. A man with the face of a fallen angel, hell-bent on practising his sorcery on unsuspecting women. A man with a voice so hypnotic she wondered if he'd practised that precise cadence and for how long before he'd attained that perfect sizzling-you-to-your-toes note that accompanied each faintly accented word.

He was the kind of man who was everything her mother had always yearned for and never achieved. The exact type of man Goldie had sworn off after witnessing time and again the way they used their God-given attributes mercilessly.

Goldie didn't hate *all* men. But she drew a particular line at playboys with enigmatic eyes and captivating faces that defied adequate description and bodies to match. Throw in the type of wealth and raw power this man next to her exuded and her warning bells clanged loud enough to be heard on the Long Island Sound.

So what was she doing in his car?

Goldie frowned, then answered her own question. Circumstances had forced her into it. But that didn't mean she wasn't still in control. Of her mental faculties *and* of her body. That zing she'd felt when he'd secured her seat belt had been a temporary aberration. The whole last hour had been a surreal sequence of events she intended to put behind her as soon as possible.

She glanced at him from the corner of her eye. When she was certain his phone had absorbed his attention, she turned and stared at his profile.

Seriously, he was like a Roman statue she'd once seen at the Museum of Natural History when she'd visited with her mother. Their trip had occurred on one of the rare times when her mother had been sober and coherent enough to make the visit. They'd stared at the statue for what had felt like an eternity, absorbing its unspeakable beauty. Her mother had sighed wistfully before her eyes had filled with tears.

Goldie had known what those tears were about. What they were *always* about. Wishes unfulfilled. A past thrown away because she'd made the wrong choices. The biggest one of which had been letting Goldie's father get away. A lump had risen to Goldie's throat as she'd watched her mother stare hard at the statue, wishing it was flesh and blood.

It had been a fruitless wish, of course.

Except Gael Aguilar was a living, breathing version of that statue.

A version who turned his head and stared straight at her in the next moment, blasting her with long-lashed light hazel eyes. Goldie attempted to look away, but for some stupid reason she couldn't drag her gaze from him.

'This proposition of yours...what's it got to do with your occupation?'

The scrape in her palm was filthy and stinging badly. Enough that it made unclenching her hand difficult. She dropped her other hand from her ripped sweater long enough to pull the business card from her pocket. It read *'CEO, Atlas Group'*. She'd made it her business to research every TV and movie production company in New York, Hollywood and Canada, just so she wouldn't miss any opportunities that might whisper past the hallowed halls of Othello. She'd never heard of Gael Aguilar's company.

'It's a new arm of my company.'

'So you were trolling the halls looking for guinea pigs?' she asked.

For some reason that amused him. Both sides of his sensual mouth lifted. Even that small action lightened his face in a way that made her breath catch. Made her wonder what it would be like to be the recipient of a full, genuine smile.

'We really need to get off the subject of animal ref-

erences. I'm a man. You're a woman. Let's refer to ourselves as such, *si*?' he drawled with a raised brow.

Something in his gaze made her self-conscious. She
cursed silently when heat rushed up to redden her face.
Because of her chosen career she'd needed to train herself not to blush at the drop of a hat, and yet she was
doing just that, simply at the droll, slightly mocking
look in his eyes.

'My question still stands,' she sniped, to cover her
uneasiness.

'And it will be answered in the fullness of time. I
need your undivided attention for that discussion.'

'What makes you think you don't have that now?'

'You mean in between trying to hang on to your
modesty and the swelling of your hand?' he enquired,
his tone almost gentle.

For some reason that made something tighten in her
midriff. Before she could form a disagreeable response
he was leaning forward. He snagged a bottle of water
from the well-stocked bar at his side of the car. Snap-
ping the plastic top free, he wet a handful of tissues
and turned to her.

'May I?' he requested, again in that gentle voice
she didn't want to associate with him. Men like him
weren't gentle. Men like him were predators, only intent on taking, taking, *taking* and leaving behind cal-
lously discarded husks.

Goldie wanted to refuse on principle, in solidarity
with her poor mother and with the bitterness that sometimes spilled into her just from being close to it. She
didn't doubt that her mother's bitterness had stained

her in some way, made her wary of certain types of men. Men like the casting director from today's audition, for instance.

She silently shook her head, veering away from the subject even while admitting she was old enough to know some of the blame for her mother's current circumstances came from Gloria Beckett herself. It took two to tango, after all.

Tango.

Okay, she wasn't going to allow an image of her tangoing with this man to cloud her already dizzying thoughts. Determinedly she clenched her gut against any more fanciful thoughts and held out her right hand.

Gael Aguilar cupped her hand in his. Goldie forced herself to ignore the alarming tingling where they touched and watch clinically as he cleaned her wound as best as the meagre supplies allowed. He worked quickly and efficiently, his manner gentle but firm. When he was finished, he disposed of the tissues and eyed her with a steady look.

'Better?'

She tested the flexibility in her hand and gave a short nod. 'Yes, thank you.'

'You see, we're not above civility after all, Miss Beckett.'

Despite the amusement in his voice there was a thin veil of something else in there…something she couldn't pinpoint. Or perhaps she wasn't willing to pinpoint it?

She'd puzzled over this man for far longer than common sense dictated was wise. 'Are we there yet?' she asked instead, then cringed at the juvenile question.

His amusement increased.

Certain he was about to make another joke at her expense she hurried to add, 'I don't have all night.' She glanced at her watch, her heart lurching when she realised the time. 'In fact, I don't think I can do this thing tonight after all. I need to be somewhere else.'

Her mother needed only the smallest excuse to regress into depression and fall off the wagon. Goldie had assured her she'd be home by ten. Any later and her mother would fret. Fretting would inevitably lead to her seeking solace at the bottom of a bottle. Goldie could only pray that her mother had fallen asleep watching TV tonight.

'You need to be somewhere else? And you didn't think to mention that before you got into my car?' His amusement had vanished. Light hazel eyes narrowed incisively on her. 'Is this some sort of game?'

'Excuse me?'

'Are you wasting my time, Miss Beckett?'

Irritation rushed up her spine. 'With respect, *you* insisted on this meeting. Granted, I'm curious to find out just what this *proposition* is, but I hadn't realised how late it was—'

'And suddenly you need to be somewhere else? You have someone waiting for you, perhaps? Boyfriend?' His gaze dropped to the hand curled into her lap. *'Husband?'*

The word held a sneer that stiffened her back, and again she caught that look in his eyes. As if he held her far below his normal regard.

Puzzlement and that growing irritation made her

frown. 'That really isn't your business, is it, Mr Aguilar? Are you in the habit of interrogating your potential business colleagues like this? It *is* business you intend to discuss with me, isn't it? If not, then I suggest you let me out right now—because I wouldn't want to waste more of your time!'

His jaw flexed for a second before his expression turned neutral. Eyes that had been mocking and mildly amused became opaque. 'It *is* a business proposition. If you need to be elsewhere, then so be it. But will you be able to live with yourself if you don't find out whether this is an opportunity you want to miss or not?'

There was a taunt in those words. There was also a look in his eyes as if he wasn't sure whether he wanted her to say yes or no.

'Does that line usually work for you?'

A sculpted eyebrow went up. 'What line?'

'The "do things my way or you'll kick yourself for ever" scam?'

He gave a half-sigh, half an irritated huff. 'I grow tired of this vacillating. You have one minute to say yes or no. Starting right now.'

He had the temerity to stare pointedly at his watch.

Dear God, she really *had* fallen down a rabbit hole! She thought she'd hit bottom with the sleazy proposition from that casting director this afternoon. It still made her skin crawl. But had she merely fallen into another dimension? One where the person making a proposition wasn't even certain whether he wanted his offer accepted or not, but went ahead and dared her to consider it anyway?

About to shake her head to clear it, she saw his eyes sharpen.

'Make up your mind, Miss Beckett. We're here.'

Goldie looked out of her window. Sure enough, they'd pulled up in front of one of those flashy-looking high-rises that dotted the Manhattan skyline. This one came complete with liveried doorman, shiny awning, and a uniformed concierge behind an imposing reception desk.

She redirected her attention to the man whose posture held more than a whiff of impatience and arrogance. 'Twenty minutes. That's all I have.'

His mouth thinned. 'We shall see.'

About to ask him what he meant, she found her words choked off when he opened his door and alighted, then turned to hold out his hand.

She didn't want to touch him. Not after the way it had felt the last time. And because she didn't want to let go of the tear in her top that showed half her boob. She shifted along the seat, and was debating how to exit with as much dignity as she could muster when he reached in and scooped her out as if she weighed nothing.

'What are you— Put me down!' she spluttered, outrage filling her as he marched her through the double doors being held open by the doorman and into a waiting lift.

He set her down and immediately the doors slid shut. The whole thing had happened in less than two minutes, and yet Goldie felt as if she'd just experienced the headiest, longest rollercoaster ride of her life. Impressions of heat, masculine scent, tensile strength, strong capable arms and…absurdly…above all, safety, buffeted her as she stared at him in astonishment from her side of the lift space.

Once he'd pressed the button for the penthouse he stepped back with a cool look. 'You said twenty minutes. I wasn't about to have the time eaten away while you decided which leg to use to exit the car.'

'My God, you're insane!' Or maybe *she* was. She hadn't been given the chance to dissect things properly yet.

His jaw flexed and his hands were rammed into his pockets. 'Far from it, *querida*. Someone has to remain rational in what is fast turning into a farce. Tell me— do you always make a huge production out of every small decision?'

'You don't know me well enough to label me a drama queen, Mr Aguilar.'

Suddenly the air in the lift thickened. The glance he levelled at her held the heavy weight of judgement. 'I've seen enough to reach a conclusion, I think.'

'What's that supposed to mean?' she countered.

One hand emerged from his pocket long enough to wave her away. 'We will not waste time discussing inconsequential subjects.'

'Do you go out of your way to ride roughshod over *everyone* you meet, or am I the lucky recipient of your special attention?'

He shrugged, sent her a sardonic whisper of a smile and exited the lift, once again leaving Goldie looking at him askance.

She followed him out, then drew to a halt when the

double doors before them were flung open to reveal a stocky Italian with twinkling brown eyes, shoulder-length hair and a wide grin.

'Gael! *Amico!* You're here. Now my night is complete.' His gaze swung to Goldie, looked her over, and his grin dimmed a touch. 'Okay, this is...interesting. My friend, do you care to tell me why your plus one is in this state? I trust you implicitly, of course, and I'm sure in a fight you'd come out the winner, but I'm not averse to attempting to kick your butt if you had something to do with the lady's um...state...'

'"The lady" is standing right in front of you,' Goldie offered with a saccharine smile. 'And trust me, she's quite capable of answering for and defending herself.'

The man's concerned look dissolved, to be replaced by the wide smile again. 'Of course. Tell me your tale, sweet one, and allow me to vanquish those that need vanquishing.'

Goldie felt a reluctant smile tug at her lips. 'I'm fine. Really. And it wasn't...your friend's fault.'

'So he was your rescuer?' the Italian asked hopefully.

'I wouldn't stretch it that far.' She looked at the man in question to see mockery and a tight little smile playing at his lips.

'*Sì*, Pietro, we're still trying to work out the finer details of our...association. But perhaps if you would be so kind as to point out the bathroom Goldie can clean up?'

Pietro nodded. 'Of course, of course. Come with me.'

He led them through the double doors and immediately turned into a bright hallway. Goldie got an impression of grey and gold decor, loud but not intrusive music, and lots of laughter coming from the living room before Gael Aguilar's presence beside her grabbed her focus. He really was imposing. And taller than she'd thought in the alley. As for those broad shoulders—

'Here you are.' Pietro turned a door handle and nudged it open to reveal a large bedroom. 'The bath room is through there. You should have everything you need. If not, please let me know.'

Goldie found another small smile. 'Thank you.'

'Prego.' Pietro returned her smile, then with a nod at Gael walked away.

Gael remained, his eyes on her. Her senses began to jump and dip in that alarming way again.

'I'm fine to take it from here,' she said, when he made no move to leave.

He made an impatient sound. 'I think we've established that I'm not going to attack you, Miss Beckett. Accepting my help won't dislodge your feminine inde pendence. Besides, trying to see to your wound with your non-dominant hand is going to eat into my twenty minutes. Unless you want to restart the clock?'

Goldie pressed her lips together, wanting to be annoyed with him for the way he made her feel a touch ridiculous. But, short of telling him she tended to refuse help from men like him on principle alone, thus probably seeming even more ridiculous despite her beliefs, she couldn't think of how to counter his assertion.

'Okay, thanks.' The words came out far too easily. Her brain knew it and her accelerating heartbeat acknowledged it as he stepped into the room and shrugged off his jacket.

His navy shirt clung to thick, sleek muscle as he flung the jacket away and moved towards the bathroom. She followed slowly, trying to hold at bay the sensation of orbiting close to a ravenous vortex.

She arrived in the spacious bathroom to find him setting out first aid materials on the double-width vanity unit. When he had finished he started to fold back his shirtsleeves.

Goldie tried to look away from strong, brawny forearms feathered with dark wispy hair as they were revealed. But the urge was hard to resist.

Her breath caught lightly as he glanced behind him and cocked his head at her.

'Come to the sink. We'll wash your wound properly before I apply some antiseptic.'

She joined him at the sink, taking care not to stand too close when his presence registered so insistently next to her. Gael Aguilar was dominating. His body seemed to vibrate with a force field that mercilessly drew every living thing into its orbit.

He turned on the taps, tested the temperature, then held out his hand. Recalling the tingling when he'd touched her in the car, Goldie wanted to refuse. But this silly dance had gone on long enough. She needed to get this over with and go back to her life. Her mother.

Thoughts of Gloria spurred her on.

She gave him her hand and once again he cupped it in his. And once again the tingling started. Only this time the sensation was twice as intense. Whether it was to do with the bright lights of the bathroom, which cast their skin to skin contact in a vivid tableau, or with the fact that he was much closer to her than he'd been in the car, she wasn't sure. All she knew was that touching Gael, having his thumbs move across her palm as he rinsed the angry gash, was like nothing else she'd ever felt.

When her breath felt strangled the sound was audible in a silence marred only by their mingled breathing. Like in the car, his movements were gentle. But the fire he created with his fingers was not. Growing alarmingly short of breath, Goldie wanted to snatch her hand from his. But then he made a sound. And she looked up. Their eyes met in the mirror. She forgot to breathe all together.

Gael's eyes had grown darker, stoked with a dark fire that made her belly clench tight. Recognising the feeling as her first ever genuine sexual attraction, Goldie gasped. His gaze dropped to her parted mouth. Stayed riveted until the almost visceral stare made her lips twitch with a need that bordered on alien.

Beneath the running tap his hands continued to caress hers. But neither of them moved their gazes except to drift them over each other's faces, returning over and over again to their mouths.

She wanted to kiss him. Be kissed by him. Now.

Her lips parted.

Gael made a sound beneath his breath. A guttural, primitive sound. And he broke his gaze from hers.

Released from the power of that rabid scrutiny, Goldie gulped greedily on the air flowing back into her lungs. Along with even more alarm at what had just happened. The thoughts she'd entertained, the want coursing through her...

Dear God... What's wrong with me?

After that sordid, grossly insulting proposition the casting director had flung her way this afternoon, sex should be the last thing on her mind. It should be buried even deeper than normal, beneath the tight, rigid focus of her ambition and her need to make something of herself. Her need not to end up like her mother—a slave to her sexual needs and emotional wellbeing, dependent on others for her happiness.

And yet here she was, letting this man touch her, trail his long fingers over her skin as if he were caressing a lover. And she…she *liked* it.

She withdrew her hand abruptly, almost knocking it against the side of the sink in her haste to dislodge the electricity his touch created.

'I… Thanks. Can we get on with it now, please?' she said, avoiding another look into those burnished gold eyes.

He muttered something beneath his breath in Spanish. But he snagged a hand towel and wrapped it around her hand before he drew her to the vanity unit.

'Sit down.'

The order was firm enough to put her back up, but she wasn't in the mood to argue any longer so she sat down where he indicated and held out her now slightly less throbbing hand.

The antiseptic stung, made her wince.

'Are you okay?' he enquired, in a deep, low voice.

Goldie wanted to look up, felt almost compelled to look into those eyes again, but she forced her gaze to remain on the clinical movements of his medical attention.

'Yes, thank you.'

He completed the cleansing, then applied a light bandage over her palm. Her hand felt a million times better by the time he was finished.

'Now for your head.'

'What?'

He held up another cotton bud. It was then that Goldie registered the slight throb at her temples. Something like relief poured through her. Then she silently grimaced at being *glad* of the minor head injury. The small gash which Gael was now cleaning didn't really explain her temporary lapse of control or the low hum through her veins. But she clung to it as the cause just the same.

Once he was done he stepped back. His gaze dropped to the hand she still had on the wide tear in her sweater. A hand growing numb from holding the torn garment in place.

'What are we going to do about this?' he enquired

She bit her lip, recognising that she couldn't very well go out into the party with a rip in her sweater. The ripped tights she could take care of by removing and disposing of them. But the tattered sweater would stand out—and not in a good way.

'I... I couldn't impose on you to find me a sewing kit, could I?' she ventured.

His eyes widened a touch, dark gold lightening to its natural hazel colour as mockery returned. 'I sincerely doubt Pietro would have something so domestic lying about. But I will do my best.'

He balled the hand towel he'd used and threw it into the laundry bin before he left the bathroom.

His departure infused the room with a lot more oxygen and a lot more clarity.

Goldie jumped off the vanity unit and stared at herself in the mirror. Besides the notable evidence of her tussle with the mugger, she didn't look as horrid as she felt. But she had lost her phone, the little money she had and, more importantly, all the details of the casting directors and agents she'd planned to contact in the hope of landing a job.

Her last paying job had been an infomercial three weeks ago, which had paid enough to sustain her and her mother's bills for another month. Her mother's part-time job as a waitress paid very little. Things were getting more than a little tight.

She'd gone into today's audition with more hope than expectation. When it had gone well she'd allowed herself to hope even harder. Until her hopes been dashed by the slimy words rolling off the director's tongue.

'My hotel room. Nine p.m. Perform well between the sheets and I'll make your dreams come true.'

Goldie had barely managed to stop herself from being sick before she ran out of the auditorium and into the bathroom. Locking herself in a stall, she'd been ashamed of the tears she'd allowed to fall. But she was proud that she had picked herself up and returned to the music room to practise her singing. She wouldn't give up because of one casting director who gave his profession a bad name. She couldn't afford to.

Taking a deep breath, she tugged off her boots and cleaned them with tissues, then finished tidying herself up as best she could. Spotting a dressing gown hanging behind the door, she quickly took off her clothes, disposed of the ripped tights and shrugged on the gown. She was securing the belt around her waist when Gael knocked.

Self-consciousness assailed her, even though the gown draped her from shoulder to ankle. Sucking in a deep breath, she opened the door.

What Gael Aguilar held out to her was most definitely not a sewing kit. 'My assumption was correct, it seems. This will have to do instead. Courtesy of Pietro's absent niece.'

Goldie eyed the scrap of material in his hand. The black cloth had probably started life in a designer's imagination as what a dress looked like. But even without examining it too closely she could tell it would be too small. On some level she knew Gael was probably trying to help. But the man's presence aggravated her on such a raw, subliminal level that she shook her head firmly in refusal. 'No, I don't think this will work.'

His mouth firmed. 'Go against your wish to fight me on every front, Miss Beckett, and just try it on. You might be surprised. Unless you wish to join the party in that dressing gown?'

Since that was out of the question, she bit back a grimace and took the dress. Eyeing the garment, she fingered the label, her breath catching slightly when she caught sight of the exclusive designer name. 'Okay, I'll wear it.'

She'd expected her acquiescence to draw another mocking response from him. Instead a hard look settled in his eyes.

'I'm glad you find *something* agreeable. Try not to keep me waiting too long, *si*?' he drawled.

Goldie shut the door without responding. She suspected dealing with a man like Gael Aguilar would be trying enough at the best of times. Add the circumstances of their meeting, and the fierce awareness that showed no signs of abating whenever they were in close proximity… She admitted that her spinning senses weren't up to dealing further with the torrent of emotions he elicited.

Returning the gown to its hook, she stepped into the dress and tugged the inch-wide straps onto her shoulders. One look in the mirror drew a gasp. The material was luxuriously elastic enough to accommodate her curves but still give her room to breathe. Reluctantly fingering the hem that ended at mid-thigh, she admitted it looked spectacular, and it felt like heaven next to her skin. But the back…

Goldie eyed the exposure of her skin from nape to waist and swallowed deeply. No way could she carry off wearing her bra with this dress. Heat rushed into her cheeks as she took a deep breath and unclipped her bra. Stuffing it into the vanity unit drawer, she grabbed her boots and tugged them on. Their familiarity brought a touch of balance and, after combing her hands through her hair again, she turned and opened the door.

He was standing at the far side of the bedroom, his surprisingly brooding gaze focused out of the French windows onto the New York night skyline.

Goldie walked in and drew to a halt in the middle of the room, her gaze once again homing in with almost helpless intent on the man who leaned with such loose-limbed indolence against the wall.

His head turned and his gaze hooked on hers before his scrutiny dropped. His sharp inhalation echoed through the room as he took her in, the hands in his pockets visibly bunching as he straightened abruptly.

And stared.

Sexual awareness, now recognised as the potent substance it was, was unstoppable as it lanced her. Intensified just from the look in his eyes.

Beneath the expensive silk and elastic blend heat suffused her, rushing through her body in a maddening dash she had no hope of stopping. But she tried. Heaven help her, she had to. Or she'd lose her mind.

Slicking her tongue desperately over her lower lip, she cleared her throat. 'I'm ready to hear your proposition now, Mr Aguilar.'

CHAPTER FOUR

THE HEATED LOOK didn't abate in his eyes. But her words, like so many others tonight, seemed to trigger a response within him.

A negative one this time.

After a few charged seconds his expression grew shuttered, and his aura when he approached her vibrated with repressed emotions she couldn't place her finger on.

'Gael,' he clipped out as he passed her and headed for the door.

'Excuse me?'

'My name is Gael. I prefer it to Mr Aguilar. Use it.'

'That sounds curiously like an order,' she replied.

He stopped abruptly, turned to face her. A deep sustaining breath lifted his chest before he speared her with his incisive gaze. 'We've both had a trying day, Goldie. Can we attempt to make it slightly *less* trying before we part ways?'

She was sure it was the use of her name, spoken so smoothly, so sizzlingly, that drew the fight from her, made her lift one shoulder in a feeble shrug. 'Sure, I can try.'

'Gracias,' he intoned. Then added, 'Thank you.'

'Um…no problem.'

A tinge of amusement lit his eyes before he shook his head. '"No problem" aren't words I associate with you.' He abruptly held up one hand. 'Not that I want to test the theory right now. Come, we shall get a drink and find a place to hold our discussion, yes?'

At her nod he resumed his exit, slowing his long stride to accommodate hers.

They entered a large, rectangular living room, decorated with a severely modern and minimalist hand. The centrepiece of the room was the futuristic-looking light fixture that seemed to take up almost a quarter of the ceiling space. Beneath this gleaming white and silver masterpiece Pietro's guests laughed and mingled. The man himself was the centre of attention, surrounded by a coolly elegant circle of females.

His grin widened when he spotted them approaching, and he beckoned them with open arms.

'Ah, there you are. Confirmation of our adventures in the Andes is needed, my friend. Sadly, I don't think these fine ladies here believe a word I'm saying!' he said to Gael.

Gael's gaze drifted over the ladies in question, who sparkled and preened even harder under his attention. Although he smiled, Goldie noticed the mirth didn't touch his eyes. Not that the action didn't have the desired devastating effect. Almost without exception every woman in the group strained towards him, their gazes rabidly checking him out.

'That particular pleasure will have to wait, my friend.

I have more important things to attend to right now.'
He turned to the waiter who had appeared next to him
and snagged two glasses of champagne.

Goldie dragged her attention from the nearest fawning woman to shake her head as he offered her one of
the glasses. 'No, thank you. I don't drink.'

She caught more than one woman sniggering.

Pietro frowned, his features almost comical with
alarm. 'You don't drink? You're not underage, are you?'

'No, I'm old enough to drink, but I choose not to,'
she repeated.

Her mother's dependency on alcohol to get her
through tough times and the depressing consequences
when that crutch failed to work had taught Goldie at a
very early age never to go near the stuff.

His eyes turning speculative, Gael returned both
drinks to the tray and steered her outside towards a
bar set up on the terrace. After taking her order for an
apple spritzer and getting mineral water for himself, he
led her to a quiet part of the hardwood floored space.
Between two tree-sized ferns a white sofa had been set
up beneath a heated lamp, which threw a lovely warm
glow over the area.

'Why don't you drink alcohol?' he asked abruptly
once they were seated.

'Do I have to have a specific reason?' she prevari-
cated.

He shrugged. 'Most people tend not to do it for two
reasons—a natural aversion or an active life choice
stemming from experience. I want to know which ap-
plies to you.'

Her fingers tightened around her chilled glass. 'Why?'

'Because one reason doesn't require further explanation, but the other might warrant further discussion if we're to work together.'

'So you're saying if I happen to be a recovering alcoholic it may ruin my chances at this imaginary job I'm yet to hear about?'

'I'm saying situations and flaws can be dealt with if they're known up front. I don't want to be blindsided by issues further down the line.'

'Mr Aguilar—'

His jaw tightened—a tiny movement, but she saw it nevertheless.

'Gael,' he intoned.

'Gael.' She stopped, unwillingly savouring the name on her tongue. Wanting to say it again. She cleared her throat and forced out a laugh. 'We seem to be getting way ahead of ourselves. Can we start this whole thing over? Please?' She held out her hand. 'I'm Goldie Beckett, graduate of Othello with honours in Acting and Musical Art. Currently unemployed and, yes, looking for a job.'

Gael stared at her hand. That mockery was swirling through his eyes once more.

After a beat, he took her bandaged hand in a firm but gentle hold. 'Gael Aguilar. My accolades are too numerous to name, but suffice it to say I'm in a position to make your dreams come true.'

Ice drenched her. She snatched her hand from his as words from earlier in the day, albeit without the sleazy overtones, fell into her lap.

His expression turned brooding. 'Something wrong?'

'Yes. You presume to know what my dreams are when you don't know me from a stranger in the street.'

'You just stated that you are unemployed. My response only pertains to an attempt to reverse that. Unless you wish to remain in a state of unemployment?'

She swallowed the bile of distaste the reminder of the day's earlier events had elicited and attempted to remain calm. 'I'm sorry. You mentioned before that you'd seen some of my audition this afternoon. I didn't notice you there, I must admit. Did you...did you see all of it?' She fervently prayed that he hadn't witnessed the sleazy exchange with the casting director immediately following the audition.

'I saw enough to make up my mind. Enough to make me return to find you.'

She lifted her glass and took a sip of her drink, her mind frantically ticking over. If he'd seen enough of her performance to make him hunt her down, then did she dare think he'd only seen the acting part, not the unsavoury denouement?

'You have a part you want me to play?' she queried, making sure to bleed her voice of hope.

It was that vulnerable hope that the casting director had exploited this afternoon, to make that demand of her. She planned not to let this man even close to the feverish hope burning in her heart.

'I have a part I *potentially* want you to play,' he amended. 'Subject to a few stipulations. And the usual auditions, of course.'

'Stipulations?'

He nodded, the light bouncing off his jet-black wavy hair. 'Very rigorous stipulations.'

'Such as?'

'We will discuss them later. Right now the broader questions concern your availability and your commitment to a long-term film project.'

Her heart skipped a beat, despite her promise to herself not to let hope take over. 'What's the role and how long are we talking about?'

'Female lead in a psychosexual thriller. Three to four months, travelling all over the world.'

Excitement fizzed through her blood. 'I'll need to read the script.'

'You'll be given a full synopsis to familiarise yourself with the story. But first you need to tell me whether you're free.'

About to say yes, she stopped when her mind veered to her mother. Despite the fierce ambition burning in her heart, the thought of leaving her mother on her own for four months made her heart lurch. But at the same time she knew this was what her mother wanted for her.

Goldie just hoped that pride in her daughter would make Gloria stick to the straight and narrow.

She returned her attention to Gael's face and experienced a slight chill at his expression. 'I'm sure I can work something out.'

One side of his mouth ticked with a hard twitch. 'Time to put your cards on the table, Goldie. Are you married?' he asked in a clipped voice.

She frowned. 'What? No.'

'Do you have a lover or a partner who will be displeased at your long absence from home?'

'I...no.'

His eyes narrowed. 'That hesitation doesn't fill me with confidence. I prefer *not* to start any association with lies.'

Affront stiffened her jaw. 'I'm not lying. The person I'm concerned about is my mother. I still live at home. With her. And she's...'

'She's what?'

She swallowed. 'Fragile.'

'In what way?'

'In ways I prefer not to divulge until something—if anything—comes out of this discussion. But I'll make sure, if it comes to it, that my home life doesn't interfere with my job.'

Silence ticked by as he stared at her. 'You're ambitious,' he drawled, with a touch of censure that grated over her skin.

'You say that like it's a bad thing. Did you not get where you are today by pursuing *your* ambition?'

He nodded. '*Sí*, but I've come to learn there are various types of ambition.'

She opened her mouth to answer, but a church clock nearby chimed, reminding her of the lateness of the hour. Whatever Gael's views on her ambitions were, they'd have to wait to be discussed some other time.

She placed her glass on a nearby table and stood up. He rose up before her, effectively blocking her from leaving.

'Where are you going? We haven't finished talking.'

She dragged her gaze from his broad shoulders and imposing body to meet his gaze. 'I can prolong our meeting, but first I'll need to call my mother. I was just going to ask Pietro if I could use his phone.'

His mouth compressed for a second, then he reached into his pocket and brought out a sleek, ultra-modern-looking phone. One she hadn't yet seen on the market. Not that she paid much attention to such trendy luxuries.

'Use mine.'

He placed the phone in her hand. She swiped her hand across the screen. Nothing happened. He cupped her hand and performed something magical with his fingers. The phone buzzed to life.

'How may I help you, Gael?' a sultry voice queried.

Goldie's eyes widened as he sent her a sly smile. 'Guest call coming up,' he said into the phone. Then he held it up to her.

'Speak the number into it and you'll be connected. When you're done with your call come and find me.'

He left her alone on the terrace and headed back inside as she recited the number of her next-door neighbour. The time on the phone read just gone ten p.m. If by some miracle her mother was asleep, the last thing Goldie wanted to do was wake her.

Mrs Robinson, on the other hand, rarely slept, and was always glued to her TV screen, watching her favourite shows. Sure enough, the old woman answered her phone on the third ring.

'Mrs Robinson, it's Goldie. Do you mind checking in on my mother for me, please? I don't want to wake her if she's asleep, but I don't want her to worry—'

'Of course I will, dear. I took her a slice of peach cobbler earlier, and she said she'd be heading to bed early. I'll go and peek in on her now. If she's up I'll stay with her until you get home. If she's asleep I'll call and let you know.'

Goldie bit her lip. 'Um…you won't be able to reach me, Mrs Robinson. I lost my phone earlier tonight. My phone *and* my purse.'

'Oh, no—are you okay?'

The old woman's concern touched her heart.

'I'm fine, thanks. I'm so sorry, but do you mind checking on her now, while I'm on the phone, please?'

'Of course. Hold on.'

Goldie breathed a sigh of relief as she heard the sprightly woman head for the door. Goldie had given her a key to their apartment years ago, when Mrs Robinson had offered to keep an eye on Gloria whenever Goldie was away. The arrangement had helped Goldie maintain peace of mind when she was at college, then later when she was out at auditions and at work.

She heard Mrs Robinson let herself in. After a minute she heard the soft snick of a door shutting.

'She's sleeping, dear. Don't worry about her. I'll keep watch. Now, what about you? Will you be okay to get home?'

Goldie hadn't quite worked it out, but she wasn't about to add to the kind old woman's burden. She looked towards the living room, where the party guests milled around, some spilling out onto the terrace to enjoy the view. Gael Aguilar wasn't one of them. When she found herself searching harder for him, she abruptly averted her gaze.

Crossing her fingers, she told a little white lie. 'I'm with a friend at the moment. I'll be fine.'

'All right. I'll see you later, honey.'

Goldie pulled the phone from her ear, not sure how to hang up. When the phone went dark she assumed it had shut itself off. She looked up to find one of the women who'd been in Pietro's circle smiling at her from the bar.

Only her smile held a whole lot of speculation. The green-eyed kind.

'So, *you're* with Gael, are you?' The slight slur, figurative and literal, was hard to miss.

Goldie forced herself not to bristle. 'No, not really.'

The blonde took her answer as an invitation to stroll closer. Expensive perfume and the faint traces of alcoholic over-indulgence reached Goldie's nostrils.

'No? If you're not together then why hasn't he been inside with us?' she demanded.

Goldie glanced towards the living room and shrugged. 'He's in there now, if you want to go talk to him.'

The blonde laughed—a brittle sound that spoke of more than just a passing interest in Gael Aguilar. 'This may be a time of equality and all that, but a woman still likes to be chased by a man.'

'Right. Okay.'

Wanting an end to the conversation, Goldie searched for her glass, only to find it had disappeared—probably taken by one of the super-attentive waiters dotted around the place. Sure enough, one of them saw her drinkless state and darted towards her with an eager smile and a tray full of drinks.

Goldie started to shake her head. 'No, thanks. I don't—'

'She doesn't drink,' the blonde stage-whispered to the waiter. When he started to turn away she stopped him with a hand on his arm. 'Wait, this is fruit punch, isn't it?' She indicated a pink drink with a gaily coloured umbrella and a straw sticking out of it.

The waiter nodded. 'Yes, ma'am.'

The blonde snagged the glass and held it out to Goldie. 'Here you go. Problem solved.'

Goldie took the drink, having no intention of drinking it. Her smile grew stiffer as the blonde examined her critically from head to toe.

'Interesting boots.'

Again, the observation came with a smile that was meant to take some of the sting out of her words.

'Interesting…dress,' Goldie replied.

Her unwanted companion laughed. 'You have a spine. I'm Heidi, by the way. And if you weren't here with the man who broke my heart last year—the man who now looks at me like we've never even met before, never mind *dated*—I'd almost like you.'

Something tiny but sharp lodged itself in Goldie's side. 'You and Gael were an item?' she asked, even though she told herself she didn't care about the answer.

Heidi's nose wrinkled, but Goldie saw the dart of pain in her eyes.

'An *item*? How quaint. We were *lovers*. I shared his

bed for six glorious weeks. Then I hit my inevitable use-by date and was bade, *Hasta la vista, baby*.'

'Inevitable?'

Her laugh held more of the pain that was slowly emerging from the bottom of her champagne glass. 'As regular as clockwork. No one, to date, has exceeded Gael Aguilar's famous month-and-a-half dating limit. So don't get your hopes up.'

Goldie frowned at the umbrella and the straw. 'You've got things completely wrong. I only met him tonight.'

Heidi's eyebrows went up. 'And he already looks at you like *that*?'

'Like what?' she asked, growing a little hot under the blonde's scrutiny.

'Are you *serious*?'

Uncomfortable with where the conversation was going, she lifted the drink to her mouth and took a long sip.

When Heidi continued to stare at her as if she was dim, Goldie shrugged with more than a hint of irritation. 'I really don't know what you're talking about. And I don't think you have anything to worry over… you know…if you want to…um…rekindle things?'

This time the laughter was pure white-hot bitterness. 'Second rule of dating Gael Aguilar. There is no second chance. Once he's done with you, you're finished for good.'

She took another drink, then hiccupped. Then grimaced as if she was in actual pain.

Goldie wanted to tell her to stop. That she really

didn't need to know any more unsavoury details about the man who'd come to her aid—the man who seemed taken enough by a fraction of the ten-minute performance he'd seen today to pursue her.

But Heidi was on a roll.

Goldie sipped at her drink and racked her brain for a convenient excuse even while she kept one eye on the living room doorway. Now she was sure her mother was safely asleep there was no need for her to rush back home, but she still needed to come up with a way to get home that wouldn't mean tapping into the emergency money she kept in her closet at home. She'd already used too much of it earlier this month, when her mother had been too depressed to go to work.

With each minute that passed Goldie saw her choices dwindling. It was too late to make her way back to Othello to ask to stay with one of her friends there. Just as with each passing minute she was learning way too much about Gael Aguilar. His preference in women—sleek, tall blondes. How many homes he owned—eight at Heidi's last count. His love of fast cars—immeasurable. His favourite food—authentic Spanish-made *paella*. His bedroom skills—

Um...no!

'I think I'm going to head back in now,' Goldie interrupted, before she could be made privy to gossip she didn't want to hear. 'Will you be all right?'

Heidi waved her empty glass at her. 'Of course! Go get my... I mean *your* man. Enjoy your six weeks!'

The statement ended with another hiccup that sounded uncomfortably close to tears.

Her heart went out to the woman. She started to reach out, wondering why her arm felt so heavy. 'Heidi—'

'Is everything okay here?' Gael's deep voice enquired.

They were both startled, and both swayed on their feet as they turned to face the source of their conversation. Gael reached out for her arm and Goldie gasped with surprise at the dizziness that assailed her.

But even in her confounding state she saw how he completely ignored Heidi.

'I...yes. I'm fine—'

'I thought you said you didn't drink?' came the sharp, cold query.

Goldie frowned. Or at least she attempted to. Her face suddenly felt funny. 'I don't. This is fruit punch.'

He calmly took his phone from her, then her glass, eyeing her with deep censure. 'It is fruit punch. Laced with rum and vodka.'

'Wh-*what*?' She turned her head with growing difficulty, met Heidi's unrepentant gaze. 'But you said it was...'

Too late, she realised what had happened.

Gael turned to his ex. 'Are *you* responsible for this, Heidi?' he gritted, his voice filled with black ice.

'Oh, so you *do* remember my name,' Heidi retorted waspishly.

'*Santo cielo!* Word of advice: playing stupid games like this with me is guaranteed to put you even lower in my regard. Grow up!'

Tears welled in her eyes. 'Damn it, Gael. Do you *have* to be so cruel?'

'Only when you pull stunts like this. I suggest you find a quiet place and get yourself together. Goldie—we're leaving.'

Goldie, beyond stunned at how easily and gullibly she'd fallen into such a dangerous situation, could only nod. She couldn't even summon pity or anger for the other woman as Gael led her past the avidly gossiping guests, a protesting Pietro, and back into the lift.

The buzzing in her ears and the thumping of her heart prevented her from speaking as she walked, plastered to Gael's side, to the limo. He helped her in, secured her seat belt as her mind reeled.

'Oh, God, I can't believe I was so… That she just…' She started to shake her head, then stopped abruptly when her vision swam.

'Believe it. Some people tend to regress into childish behaviour when they feel slighted. Heidi has perfected the art.'

She wanted to ask then what he'd seen in the woman to make him date her, but the question was redundant. The blonde was a goddess. And, according to her, just the type of woman Gael favoured.

The car started to move, turned a corner. Goldie slapped a hand to her mouth as her stomach roiled. When he passed her a white paper bag she grasped it gratefully.

When the car had steadied, she risked a glance at his wavering figure. 'I'm sure you think me…naive and gullible.'

She wasn't sure whether he'd shrugged or not, but his voice held a distinct bite. 'For someone who claims not to drink, I'm surprised you didn't recognise the peculiar taste straight away.'

'I wasn't… I didn't… I've never tasted vodka before. Or rum.' She grimaced. 'Does this mean I've lost my chance with you? I mean with the audition?' she ventured, feeling her tongue slurring her speech.

God, how many times had she heard her mother sound like this? And how many times had Goldie's spirits dropped with disappointment and pity?

Hard hazel eyes sliced into her. 'Just as you claimed earlier, I too have to be elsewhere tomorrow. And since I can't have a conversation with you now, in this state, I'll have to see when my schedule opens up again.'

Her fingers curled around the lowered paper bag. 'Just give it to me straight, Gael. Tell me whether I've blown it or not so we can say our goodbyes.'

'What difference will it make?'

She licked her lips, desperation beginning to claw through her. 'If I haven't blown it completely I'd like the opportunity to fix it. I… I need this job. I need *a* job!'

His nostrils flared slightly. 'And how would you propose to go about *fixing* it?'

She shook her head, then groaned. 'I don't know. Maybe you can tell me what I can do…how I can—?'

His pithy curse dried up her words.

Goldie knew then that she was digging herself deeper into the hole she'd unwittingly found herself in. It was too late. She'd messed up a shining opportunity. Through ignorance and gullibility.

She snorted, her insides shredding with disappointment and chagrin. How *could* she have fallen into the same trap she'd condemned her mother for for so many years?

'What's your address?'

'My…address?'

'My driver will deliver you home,' he stated, his voice neither gentle nor harsh.

It was almost as if he'd become indifferent to her.

Goldie fought to dismiss the slight pang that thought brought and focused on a much more troubling problem.

'I can't go home,' she muttered, the words filling her with even more distress.

'Excuse me?' His voice was filled with chilly cynicism.

She grimaced, her hand shaking as she lifted it to her numb cheek. 'I can't go home in this state.'

Gael's gaze sharpened on her face. 'Why not?'

Shame dredged deep inside her. 'I… My mother is a recovering alcoholic. I can't… She can't see me like this.'

He regarded her for several charged seconds before his jaw clenched. *'Dios mio.'*

'I know how this looks, okay?' she pre-empted, before he could voice the condemnation bristling over his frame. 'But I can't do this to her! After everything she's been through, I can't—'

'Calm yourself, Goldie. I was merely going to say I'm not blameless in all this. I should've suspected Heidi would try something like this. I shouldn't have left you on your own for so long.'

She heaved in a breath and fought the clogging in her throat. 'I… Thanks.' She clenched her unhurt hand, ashamed at how low she felt. 'I know you probably think I'm pathetic right now, but I'm responsible for my mother. If she sees me like this it'll destroy her. In many ways I've been the adult for a long time. Every choice I make...she's my number one priority.'

His mouth tightened. 'Even when the choices you make aren't sound?'

She shrugged. 'I'm not perfect. I make mistakes like everyone else. That doesn't mean I should rub her nose in it. She has enough to deal with.'

'I see.'

'*Do* you?'

'Let's not enter another debate, hmm...?'

Her eyes widened when he shoved his door open. She stared around her, not sure when the car had stopped.

'Where are we?' she asked.

'My hotel. Since you don't want to go home, you can stay here tonight,' he said.

A different emotion, separate from the ones she was already battling, fizzed through her. 'I'm not sure—'

'I'm staying in the presidential suite. Besides the master suite there are two more bedrooms. With locks. You're invited to use either one of them. If you don't feel safe enough with that, tell my driver where you'd like to go and he will deliver you to whatever destination you require,' he stated in implacable tones.

The same instinct that had told her she could trust him enough to get into his limo after the mugging told her she could trust his offer. But suddenly Goldie wasn't sure she could trust *herself*.

She'd let herself down spectacularly once tonight.

Did she dare trust that she wouldn't make another mistake on this surreal night?

But what alternative did she have that didn't involve wandering the streets in an intoxicated state, with a bullseye on her back for every creep out there?

She swallowed hard and accepted that this was the best possible, safest choice on the table.

'I accept your offer. Thank you.'

Twenty minutes later Goldie was in the most comfortable bed she'd ever slept in, the double doors to the princess suite locked after a solicitous Gael had brought her a glass of water and turned down the bed.

Now, stripped to her underwear, Goldie sighed and drifted off to sleep among the dreamiest of pillows.

CHAPTER FIVE

SHE WASN'T SURE what made her jerk awake. Perhaps it was the muted sounds of the city, when she was used to her quieter neighbourhood just outside Trenton, New Jersey. Whatever it was, once her racing heart slowed she became aware of another raging need. Thirst.

The glass Gael had left her with was empty, although she didn't recall drinking the water. She grimaced at the hazy, alcohol-distorted memories and got out of bed. She hated it that she hadn't made it home, but after what had happened Goldie knew this option was best. Her mother wouldn't have been just disappointed, she would also have blamed herself. Didn't studies show that alcoholism was sometimes hereditary? And Gloria blaming herself would only bring about one result—depression.

For the past few months her mother had been doing well. Goldie couldn't stomach being the cause of any form of regression in her mother's wellbeing.

Rising from the bed, she looked down at her scantily clad body. The thought of putting on that clingy dress again just to go and fetch a glass of water brought another grimace. Going to the adjoining bathroom, she shrugged into a dressing gown bearing a distinctive exclusive designer's monogrammed label, belted it, and left the suite with the empty glass.

Her bare feet moved silently over marbled floors as she walked along the ornately decorated hallway and into the vast living room. Styled in white, gold and royal blue, the presidential suite was the last word in elegance, right down to the hand-scrolled stationery and the monogrammed cushions that graced the brocade sofas and antique claw-footed chairs. Also dotted around the room were gilt and mother-of-pearl framed mirrors, and expensive paintings reflected perfection and elegance at each turn.

On the far side of the living room, set back from a second grouping of blue and gold-striped settees, a black baby grand piano gleamed under the lamps left on to illuminate the space. Next to it was a tiny kitchenette, housing a fridge and a collection of expensive drinks.

It was there that Goldie went to fetch bottled water. And there she remained frozen after, having taken a large gulp, she heard the heated sound of Gael's voice as he paced the private terrace outside.

She didn't want to eavesdrop, and really she didn't understand a word of the bullet-fast Spanish he spoke into the phone, but that didn't matter. She saw his pacing grow hurried as the conversation gained intensity. His fingers spiked through his hair and Goldie's breath caught as he swore beneath his breath.

She eyed the semi-dark living room.

Leaving the small alcove would reveal her presence.

But staying where she was, witnessing what appeared to be an argument—although she wasn't absolutely certain—would be a worse violation of his privacy.

Taking a deep breath, she slid her glass onto the counter and stepped out of the alcove. Just in time to hear him snarl before he ended the conversation.

Like a magnet, her gaze swung to him.

He stood frozen between the French doors, the phone tight in his grip, his eyes locked on her.

'I don't speak Spanish, so I didn't understand any of what you were saying,' she blurted.

One corner of his mouth twisted, although tightly packed anger still seethed from his tall, imposing frame. Moving forward into the room, he shut the door behind him and tossed his phone onto the counter without taking his eyes off her.

'You don't need linguistic understanding to know what's going on.'

'I guess not,' Goldie replied, her skin jumping at the sparks still lurking in his eyes. She stared at him until the breath locked in her lungs. Then she dragged her gaze away. 'Um…goodnight.'

'Are you feeling better?' he asked, and his voice contained a bite. She couldn't determine whether it was aimed at her or was residual from his phone call.

She stopped her retreat. Nodded. 'Yes, thanks.'

'Then stay. Join me for a nightcap. Yours will be water, of course.'

For some reason she felt a little bit better that a trace of mockery was back in his voice. Retracing her steps to the counter, she picked up her half-empty glass and waited for him to pour an expensive-looking cognac before she joined him on the sofa.

She noted that he still wore his shirt and trousers from earlier, although a few more buttons had been undone on his shirt, giving her a glimpse of a firm, bronze contoured chest and a strong throat.

Averting her gaze from the arresting sight, she stared around, painstakingly counting the pieces of furniture in the room as a distraction tactic.

Fifteen.

Her eyes swung back to him.

Gael was watching her. He didn't seem inclined to speak, appeared just content to sip his drink, preferring to keep his thoughts internal. Goldie licked her lips, knowing this wasn't the time to pursue the business conversation they'd begun before her inadvertent trip into Liquor Land. When his stare got too much, she glanced around again, her gaze landing on a small ornate clock on top of an antique console table.

Two o'clock in the morning. 'So, do you conduct *all* your business meetings in the early hours of the morning?'

His gaze shifted from her to the contents of his glass. 'That wasn't business. It was family,' he said, confirming her earlier suspicion.

'Family?' she intoned faintly.

'*Sí.*' That crack of a smile was at his lips again. 'You're not the only one with maternal challenges.'

'You were arguing with your *mother*?'

His mouth twisted. 'You could say that.'

'Why?'

'Because there's a problem. Isn't that why people argue?' he snapped.

She frowned. 'Well, yes, but...'

'I don't wish to talk about that, Goldie.' His voice was a low, raw command.

Knowing how *she* felt about the subject of her own mother, she nodded. 'Okay. What *do* you wish to talk about?'

'You. Why acting?' he asked, his voice cold and abrupt.

'Because I'm good at it,' she stated without arrogance.

His breath huffed in a short laugh. '*Sì*, that you are.'

He raised his glass in a toast that felt wrong. And not in the mocking way she was getting used to.

She stared at him, but couldn't read his expression. 'Gael—'

'How many auditions have you given like the one you performed today?' He cut across her.

'This was my second. The first was for a workshop in the East Village a month ago.'

'And the script? What play is it from?' he pressed.

She hesitated, unsure where he was coming from. Unwilling to have her work mocked. 'It's my own work. I wrote it last year.'

'Tell me about it.'

Goldie shrugged. 'It's a story about...resilience, dependency, trust. About two people who care for each other but can't be together because of perceived insurmountable obstacles.'

He took a sip. Swallowed. His eyes locked on her. 'What obstacles?'

She toyed with the ends of the gown's belt. 'Alcoholism. Infidelity…' she murmured.

'And the piece you performed today? Which of those two things did it deal with?'

'Both. Her alcoholism. His infidelity. He wants to give up. She wants to stay and fight.'

He stiffened, his eyes slowly narrowing. 'It sounds like they're toxic together. Don't you think they're better off apart? As far from each other as they can get?'

'Maybe they are—maybe they're not. But surely it's better to find a way through the conflict than to give up at the first hurdle? Stick it out for a while for the sake of the love that might be buried beneath all that? Surely they owe it to themselves to root through the toxicity and find it? Maybe that's what will heal them?'

She forced her voice past the lump threatening to rise in her throat.

'What if their so-called love is toxic too? And how long is "a while"? How much is enough when everyone around you has to bear the brunt of the toxicity?' he demanded.

His voice had grown ragged, raw with a frustration and anger that she knew instinctively stemmed from that phone call.

'I don't have the answers. But I know I'd never give up something that important that easily,' she said.

He stared at her, his gaze probing deep. Deeper.

'Do it,' he said, in a low, rumbling voice just a shade above a whisper.

Her breath caught. Strangled her. 'Do…what?'

'The piece. Perform it for me.'

Shock sent her rigid for a second. *'Now?'*

'We're both awake. We're here. You asked me in the car what you could do. *This* is what you can do. Show me what I want to see.'

It was clear that Gael was still affected by whatever had happened during that phone call. Talking to his mother had disturbed him badly. Enough to make Goldie consider saying no…consider questioning his objectivity.

Because this no longer felt like business. This had become something else. Something emotional. Something hot and heavy and dangerous. Perhaps even deeply personal.

But, on the flipside, it was just what she needed. She needed her audience to be emotionally invested, not clinically detached. Even if he didn't believe what she was selling, he would feel strongly about it somehow. And wasn't that a good thing?

Reaching out, she offered him the glass in her hand. His gaze went from it to her face and back again before he took it. Set it to one side.

The moment his gaze returned to her face she spoke the first lines.

'You won't leave me. I won't let you.'

'Maybe it's the best thing for me to leave.'

His raw, unexpected response made her heart race faster.

'You think you love her, but you don't.'

'Perhaps I'm not capable of loving anyone. Not even myself.'

The words were spoken with a quiet, strong convic-

tion that made her eyes widen. Made her certain she
was glimpsing something Gael Aguilar might not want
her to had circumstances been different. Had he not
been caught up in whatever emotions held him prisoner right now.

*'I don't believe that. Besides, I know you enough
to tell you what is in your heart. I love you that much,
Simon. Enough to forgive. Enough to take another
chance on us. But for us to happen you need to stay.
Please...take the chance.'*

'Even if staying is perpetuating the cycle? Destroy-
ing us and everyone else who comes into our orbit?' he
rasped, his eyes fixed firmly on her.

Tears prickled her own eyes.

Slowly she reached out and laid a hand on his. *'We'll
find a way, but we'll only find a way if we're together.
Don't leave. Please...take the chance on us. I love you.
Fight with me. Fight for us.'*

The powerful exposing words, spoken from a place
in her own personal pain—the pain of suffering a broken family—rumbled through the room, moved through
her as she blinked and raised her gaze to Gael.

The look on his face made her breath catch. It was a
mixture of pain, regret and frustration. There was also
hunger. A visceral need for connection that lanced her
from the short distance between them.

'Dios mio, you're good. So very good...' he muttered,
his tone gravel-gruff.

Between one second and the next the hand beneath
hers moved, turned and captured hers. He drained his

glass and tossed it aside. Then he used their meshed hold to drag her close.

Goldie ended up in his lap, the air knocked from her. Before she could take a needed breath Gael's mouth was on hers. Hot and sizzling and cognac-laced.

He brought every emotion bubbling beneath the surface of his skin to the kiss.

Goldie had been kissed before, either through her work or through casual acquaintance dates that had never gone anywhere. No past experience came close to what she was feeling now as Gael's lips devoured hers, slipped past her stunned senses to breach them deeper. Her hands curled into his shirt, fisted, held on tight as his tongue licked her lower lip, her upper lip, then charged inside, his intense savouring of her drawing fire through her veins, drenching her from head to toe in white-hot sensation. Need slammed hard into her, making her moan and strain closer to his tensile strength, to the heat of sleek muscles moving beneath the cotton shirt.

She slid her hands higher, closer to the exposed skin of his chest, his throat. At her first touch they both groaned. Gael dragged her closer still, his hand moving to her hips and positioning her more firmly in his lap until the bottom of her robe fell open, her legs moved to either side of him. When she was situated to his liking he speared one hand through her hair, using his hold to angle her head, fusing their mouths closer together.

The kiss was like nothing and everything she'd ever dreamed of. Goldie felt as if she was flying and drowning at the same time. Her lungs screamed with the need for oxygen. She wanted to deny their request, to just keep experiencing the incredible sensation of kissing Gael Aguilar.

Only the pressure of his hand in her hair finally broke her free. But it was only so he could set her back a scant few inches, stare up at her with a face masked in raw, edgy lust.

'I want you, Goldie. I want to have you. Right here, right now,' he rasped, low and deep, his eyes dark with ravaging hunger and fierce intent.

Beneath her, his hips flexed, his powerful erection nestling deeper between her thighs, ramming home to her the strength of his desire.

Need pounded with relentless force through her. A need she knew she should fight. But for the life of her she couldn't summon the willpower. All the same, she tried.

'Gael—'

He closed the gap between them, forcing her answer back down her throat as he kissed her again, showed her with his mouth how feeble any protest she wanted to attempt would be. Groaning, she slid her hands up his strong neck, noting the raging pulse beneath her touch, glorying in it for a second before her fingers spiked into his hair.

His guttural groan was one of encouragement. Of ferocious need. They stayed like that for endless minutes, her on top of him, kissing him as if her life depended on it.

All too soon, he forced her head back again.

'Don't deny me, Goldie. Don't deny us both,' he rasped.

His accent was more pronounced, his voice curling around the words, burning them into her skin the way his eyes burned for her.

At twenty-four, Goldie knew she was an anomaly in the virgin stakes, and would probably draw mockery from Gael if he knew the depth of her innocence. But it was an innocence she was proud of—an innocence she'd fought to retain simply because she knew what throwing it away on the wrong person would make her feel further down the line. She'd watched her mother throw her body and her emotions away on the wrong men for far longer than she wanted to dwell on.

She'd already made a mistake that might have had disastrous consequences tonight. Was she risking making another?

She sucked in a deep breath—which emerged in a rush when Gael leaned up and slowly licked her lower lip. Her whole body shook with the headiness of that bold claiming. The fingers she had locked in his hair tightened, encouraged him as he kissed the corner of her mouth, her cheek, her jaw, her earlobe.

'Let me have you, Goldie *mia*. *Por favor*,' he whispered in her ear. 'Let's turn this unfortunate night into a better one. A memorable one. I can make it so good for you.'

She groaned beneath the weight of his torrid, tempting words even as she fought to rationalise what was happening. Could she do it? Could she give herself to him for just one memorable night?

The answer burned hot and urgent beneath her skin. But Goldie ignored it for a moment, pulled her dwindling faculties together for long enough to separate what was happening here from the history she knew and had fought hard to prevent repeating.

Where her mother had fallen down had been when she'd imagined herself in love with the men who had ultimately used and betrayed her. Nothing so fanciful was happening here tonight. Gael wanted her body. She wanted his. Their needs were mutual. The only emotion present here was the hunger that demanded to be answered.

'Say yes, *mi dulce*.' He kissed her cheek one more time, then drew back to spear her with flaming eyes. 'Say *yes*.'

The word, eating her alive, burst free. 'Yes.'

His harsh exhalation preceded his forceful rise from the sofa. The moment he was upright he urged her legs around his waist. Then, with one hand banded around her, the other fisted in her hair, he made his way unerringly down the hall and into the master suite.

The room, like the rest of the penthouse, was luxury personified. Tasteful and expensive antique furniture mixed with contemporary designs to produce a breathtaking setting fit for a king.

Or for an impossibly sexy, arrogant, ravenous Spaniard, whose sole attention was fixed on her with a feverish intensity that made every single one of her senses jump in mingled excitement and trepidation.

Burnished eyes trapped her in place as he set her down and started to undo the remaining buttons of his shirt. With each further expanse of golden skin revealed her mouth and fingers tingled with the need to touch, to taste.

'Take off your robe, Goldie,' he commanded gruffly as he shrugged off his shirt and tossed it aside.

Her fingers twitched, but for the life of her she couldn't move. Because he was perfect. Not a spare ounce of flesh resided on the upper half of his body. She'd been so right to compare him to that Roman statue. His musculature was streamlined, a true work of art that filled her with awe. And with a great, demanding need.

Between her thighs her flesh pulsed with an unfamiliar urgency. An urgency so great she wondered how she was still standing.

'Goldie.' His voice was a furnace-hot warning. 'Are you deliberately keeping me waiting?'

Her head moved in a slow shake and her hand reached for the belt. 'No. I just…wanted to look at you.'

His breath was expelled harshly, almost as if she'd surprised him. Colour slashed high on his cheekbones and he closed the gap between them, speared his fingers into her hair. He angled her face up but didn't kiss her, merely traced that hot gaze over her face.

'You can look at me all you want later. Right now I want you naked and beneath me. So the robe, *bellezza* Goldie. *Take it off.*'

With quick, jerky movements she pulled the belt loose and shrugged the robe off her shoulders, leaving only her cotton panties on.

His gaze stayed on hers for a long, absorbing moment

before he slowly stepped back. His exhalation was half a groan, half an expression of wonder. The fingers of one hand traced her pulse, her collarbone, then moved down to the delicate space between her breasts. Then he moved behind her, fingers still on her skin, tracing over her shoulders to the top of her spine.

A shudder rushed over her—the beginning of many that rolled in a never-ending reaction to Gael's touch on her body. His fingers drifted down her spine, then back up again, eliciting a deep moan she was helpless to stop. In the next instant his nails were dragged lightly down her body and he groaned at her deep shudder. She swayed beneath the onslaught of fierce desire. It triggered a frenzied response and suddenly he was back in front of her, his fiery gaze moving down her body, savouring her anew.

'*Santo cielo*, you're exquisite,' he murmured huskily.

Catching her around the waist, his movements a touch uncoordinated, he tossed her onto the bed and tugged at his belt.

Goldie brushed her hair out of her eyes, the better to see him, and then almost wished she'd averted her gaze when his body was revealed in all its manly, almost intimidating glory. She swallowed hard when she took in the fullness of his manhood.

Heavens.

A trace of that arrogant smile touched his lips as he moved towards her. 'Your beautiful eyes stare a little too hard, *guapa*. Do you wish to unman me before we even begin?'

She blushed, hot and fierce, drawing a low laugh

from him. She dragged her gaze up with monumental effort. 'You're laughing, which tells me you don't think my unmanning you is a possibility.'

His laughter drifted away, replaced by deep, stark hunger. He stalked to the bed, prowled to loom over her. One finger traced over her nose to her mouth, testing the suppleness of her lower lip before he demanded entry. When she took his digit into her mouth, he groaned.

'With a woman as intoxicating as you, everything is possible.'

His kiss this time was ten times more carnal, devastatingly brutal in its hunger. Luckily Goldie was equally ravenous for this new, dizzying sensation that threatened to drown her. But she hung on, clung to Gael's broad shoulders as he took her on a frighteningly exciting journey.

Even after he broke away and started to trail his mouth down her body she was still lost in that intoxicating kiss. It was only when he reached her breasts, tweaked and sucked on the stiff, needy peaks, then dropped lower to kiss the sensitive skin below her navel, teasing her panty line with his teeth and lips, that she fell into a different but equally exhilarating dimension of pleasure.

Her panties were tugged off in quick, expert movements. Then he was parting her legs, kissing his way up her inner thighs.

Goldie didn't even attempt to halt what was coming. She wanted it all. Was greedy enough to raise herself onto her elbows, stare in wonder as he drew inexorably closer to the bundle of need between her thighs.

His gaze locked on hers in that final second before he tasted her, his nostrils flaring one last time as he drew in her essence. He muttered something hard and pithy under his breath. Then he swiped his tongue boldly across her flesh.

Her hips jerked as sensation pounded her in a merciless wave. She collapsed back against the pillows, her breath emerging in shameless pants as pleasure surged through her. When Gael found the bundle of nerves that screamed for attention she cried out, her eyes squeezing shut to savour the sensations she knew instinctively would blow her away. The pressure between her thighs increased, and his tongue flicked urgently against her flesh as he groaned through his own pleasure.

Between one breath and the next she was flung into nirvana, her mind and body no longer her own as pure bliss buffeted her. Her moan fused into one long, earthy sound, and her convulsions were endlessly thrilling.

The moment her pulse began to slow she felt him move, heard him reach across her body. She opened her eyes to see him tearing open a condom, rolling it over his impressive girth.

Goldie debated then whether to tell him that she was a virgin, that he was about to be her first. But she knew then that two things might happen.

Firstly, he might not believe her. She hadn't forgotten the occasional glimpses of censure he'd sent her way a few times since they'd met. Men like Gael had cynicism bred into their DNA. She couldn't explain any other reason for those looks.

Secondly, he might believe her and think she had an agenda in all this—a motive for giving herself to him. It couldn't be further from the truth. Theirs was to be a coupling bred solely of attraction and need. Nothing more.

So she bit her lip and forced herself to meet his gaze. Whatever he saw in her face satisfied him enough to make him lower his body to hers, to free her lip from her teeth and take her mouth in a possessive, incandescent kiss.

After an age, he lifted his head.

'Touch me, Goldie. Hold on to me when I take you. I want you to know who it is that possesses you tonight.'

The raw demand robbed her of her already short breath. 'Gael—'

'*Sí*, say my name like that. Just like that...' he commanded gruffly as he positioned himself between her legs. One hand gripped her thigh, and the other fisted in her hair. The easy strength with which he held himself poised above her was testament to his powerfully honed physique, which was a beautiful sight to behold.

His fierce arousal spoke of a different power altogether—one that made her heart palpitate with trepidation even as her senses flared in anticipation.

Remembering his instruction to hold on to him, she slid her arms around his waist, caressing the corded muscles in his lower back.

Hazel eyes darkened as they met hers. His head dropped and his mouth fused with hers as he penetrated her with one sure, focused thrust.

Her muted scream rose and died between their kiss.

But not the pain. God, not the pain. That held her rigid for a few endless seconds.

Above her, Gael's eyes flared, probed. He raised his head and stared at her. 'Goldie…?'

She wasn't sure whether it was a question or an observation. She registered her lost innocence and held on to him, unable to form words as the pain lingered, then faded to leave behind new, breath-catching sensations.

'Gael…' she murmured.

He shook his head, perhaps answering his own question. Perhaps caught in the burgeoning rapture of their union. He moved. He groaned. His head went back as he withdrew and thrust again.

'*Dios mio*, you feel sensational,' he muttered roughly.

'Gael…'

He withdrew and thrust again, his mouth dropping to hers for a searing, groan-laced kiss. 'Yes, Goldie. My name on your lips. Don't stop. I want to hear it.'

And she wanted to say it, she realised. So she did.

He set the pace—slow at first, then faster, building a conflagration within and between them that soon raged out of control. With it came a feverish need to touch, to kiss, to taste, to bite. Her nails raked and dug in as he took her higher. His fingers fisted in her hair, and he devoured her mouth as pleasure overtook them.

When the bough broke her cries mingled with his unfettered roar. Guttural words in Spanish poured from his lips as his climax pulled him under. Then Gael half collapsed on top of her, catching himself at the last moment to roll them over.

Hearts racing, they gulped air into their starving

lungs, their hands unable to stop moving over each other's sweat-coated flesh.

But eventually their heartbeats calmed. Hands stilled. Breath was restored.

Gael pulled himself free, unable to find adequate words to sum up what had happened in the last hour. He left the bed and entered the bathroom without looking at the woman whose body he'd just shamelessly gorged himself on. He wasn't usually so lacking in after-sex small talk, but for the life of him he couldn't seem to locate his tongue.

Entering the bathroom, he shut the door behind him, then leaned weakly against it. His body still thrummed with what he could only describe as the most sensational sex he'd ever had in his life. But already tendrils of regret burrowed beneath his skin.

This shouldn't have happened. Not like this. Not when the phone call with his mother and her blatant confirmation that she was once again embroiled in an affair with Tomas Aguilar had set him on the finest, most dangerous edge.

Because the mere mention of his father's name had triggered more memories. Memories that had left him deeply puzzled as to why his mother—who should know better—was once again taking this degrading path.

For Tomas Aguilar, Katerina Vega had been a salacious means to a calculated end the first time round. Tomas had admitted as much when Gael had confronted him on his twenty-first birthday. Just as he'd admitted what Gael had always been too afraid to learn—that he'd been an unfortunate consequence of that game of emotional roulette.

Personally, his illegitimacy had long ceased to distress him—simply because he didn't give it much cerebral capacity. It was a buried burr, cemented over with time and distance, and he'd learned to live with it. The taunts from his childhood were in the past, as was the village where he and his mother had been relentlessly stigmatised as outsiders and homewreckers. Even his inability to sustain a relationship past a month or two had worked out for him in the long run by diverting his focus to empire-building.

And yet all these years later he'd yet to succeed in getting that last damning statement out of his head.

'Tú estás un error...'

'You are a mistake.'

Gael knew it was partly that voiced statement that made him feel relief each time he left Alejandro's presence. His half-brother was a lot of things, but Gael knew he was not a mistake to the parents who'd created him. And while Alejandro had preceded Gael in leaving Spain, for reasons similar to his own, witnessing him taking steps to confront his past...and succeeding...left Gael still feeling an annihilating bitterness every time he thought of Tomas Aguilar.

So he'd chosen not to think of his father at all.

But now, with his mother's actions—which he was growing more convinced were of her own volition this time—he couldn't think of anything *but*!

He'd let his emotions get the better of him tonight. Perhaps even taken advantage of Goldie because of it.

Cursing, he moved from the door to the sink. About to remove the condom, he looked down. Froze. And cursed some more.

No. It couldn't be. She was in her twenties. She couldn't be a virgin. And yet the evidence of blood, the confirmation of his suspicion when he'd taken her, was glaring and unmistakable.

Dios mio.

Shock morphed into a different sensation. Had this been a trap? A way to secure a surer payday?

Disposing of the condom, he washed himself and stalked back into the bedroom, ready to confront her.

Except Goldie was curled on her side, fast asleep.

For ten minutes he paced the room, unaccustomed indecision plaguing him. Then, once he knew there was only one way to play this, he turned and headed for his dressing room.

CHAPTER SIX

THE WORST POSSIBLE CHOICE in a sea of bad choices.

She'd gone to sleep dreading those words were true but they were the first to slam across her mind the moment Goldie woke up. Because even before she opened her eyes she knew things wouldn't look better in the bright light of day.

Not after Gael had hurried away after making love to her as if hell's demons snapped at his heels.

Not after being left alone with nothing but her thoughts to occupy her.

The beginnings of doubt and disappointment at what she'd done crowded her every thought process.

The bottom line was that she'd found a neat argument to give herself permission to sleep with Gael. But in the cold light of day those arguments rang disturbingly hollow. She'd indulged herself simply because she'd been too weak to resist the temptation of the most compelling man she'd ever met.

Sure, she could forgive herself for it—eventually—but in succumbing to momentary madness had she given up more than her virginity? Had she also burned bridges in the career she'd fought tooth and nail to succeed in forging for herself? She didn't need the internet to confirm to her that Gael Aguilar had power and clout. Nor was she naive enough to think she could escape unscathed from her one mistake should he be indiscreet enough to whisper about what had happened between them.

She only had one choice. She had to talk to him—make it clear that they were to treat what had happened between them last night as the transient indulgence it was and nothing else. She wasn't above begging for his discretion if it came to that. She had too much to lose.

Turning over, she opened her eyes.

To see an empty space next to her.

She wasn't surprised to find him gone. After all he'd left her wide awake, seconds after they'd made love, and locked himself into the bathroom. Had she not been completely shattered, she would have dragged herself off to the other bedroom to avoid what must have been an even more humiliating sight for Gael when he'd emerged from the bathroom.

Had he even slept in the same bed with her? Or had he availed himself of one of the unoccupied bedrooms so he wouldn't have to look at her or deal with her? Had she been so disappointing that she hadn't merited six minutes, never mind his customary six weeks? Not that she'd intended to have that long a time with him!

Her face heated as humiliation mounted. She didn't want to acknowledge the dull pain in her chest, but Goldie was a believer in facing problems head-on. Yes, she'd given her virginity to a man who hadn't even acknowledged it. A part of her was glad of that. But another small part mourned her lost innocence because, while the experience had been phenomenal, she couldn't think about it without thinking about what had come after. Without thinking about why her chest felt tight with unsettling emotions she was too anxious to examine.

Dragging herself upright, she looked around her. The dressing gown was draped over a chair, her underwear laid on top of it. More heat surged into her face at the thought of Gael touching her things. Pushing the disturbing thought away, she rose, then gasped as her body's discomfort registered. The enormity of what she'd done grew as she gathered the clothes and made her way back to her room.

If she'd still kept the diary she'd used to as a teenager, the events of the last twenty-four hours would have been emblazoned in red ink across her trusted leather-bound notebook. But, alas, they were to be confined in a secret vault in her mind, only to be examined on the rarest of occasions at some remote point in the future, when humiliation didn't burn this bright or this painfully.

She was debating in her mind exactly when that occasion would be when she entered the other bedroom suite.

The note propped up against her pillow was hard to miss, with the hotel's distinctive burgundy and cream stationery standing out against the white sheets, and the bold black scrawl across the paper.

Trepidation eating at her, she walked across the room and plucked up the folded paper.

Goldie,
I've decided to go a different way with the dis-
cussed role. The driver will be waiting when
you're ready to take you wherever you need to
go. Take as much time as you need.
   The contents of the envelope are a token of my
gratitude for your time.
G

Even before her numb fingers had located and opened the envelope, which had been propped up behind the note, sheets of icy rage were bucketing down on her.

Yesterday Goldie had thought that casting director asking her to go to his hotel suite for sex if she wanted the role she'd auditioned for was bad enough. Now she knew the depths of true humiliation.

She wasn't even sure why she took out the sheaf of dollar bills and counted them. Perhaps she wanted to know just how much her degradation was worth to Gael Aguilar. It certainly wasn't because she intended to use a single cent of it.

Ten thousand dollars.

Hot, humiliating tears filled her eyes. When they dripped down her cheeks she angrily swiped them away. Was this how her mother had felt each time she was used and discarded?

Goldie wasn't proud that she'd inadvertently walked in her mother's shoes. But she hadn't done it through choice. She didn't deserve this!

Her anger wiping away the last of her humiliation, she dressed in last night's clothes, uncaring of how she'd look walking across the famous hotel's lobby. Her rage would insulate her just fine.

She stopped in the bathroom long enough to wash her face and tidy her hair before she exited the suite, the note and the envelope full of cash clutched tight in her fist.

A butler of indeterminate age emerged as she entered the lavish living room. 'Good morning, miss. Would you like some breakfast?' he asked in cultured tones.

Putting on her best acting skills, she smiled and shook her head. 'No, thank you. Is it possible to summon the driver?'

'Of course, miss. Would you like me to tell him the destination or would you prefer to relay it yourself?'

'I'll take care of it. Thank you.'

The butler nodded and crossed over to a nearby phone. After a short conversation he returned. 'He's pulling up now, miss. If you'd allow me to escort you…?'

He led her out to the private marble-floored foyer and into the lift that solely served the presidential suite. Stepping in with her, he swiped a gold access card and pressed the button for the ground floor. Goldie was thankful for his discretion as they exited onto a side street that led to Fifth Avenue, but she couldn't stop herself from wondering how many times this butler-driver scene had been staged to facilitate Gael's predilection for one-night stands.

The very thought filled her with even more distaste and anger, darkening her mood as she emerged into the sunlight.

The limo was parked only steps from the revolving

doors, its driver standing attentively at the back door. He tipped his hat when he saw her, his face politely neutral.

Goldie hated herself for the lie she was about to tell, but she would never be able to live with herself if she let this go unchallenged. She couldn't bear the thought that Gael Aguilar would reside in his lofty kingdom, content that he'd bought and paid for her and was therefore free of wrongdoing. So she waited until the butler had retreated before she faced the driver and waved the scribbled note.

'Gael left me a message that you were to take me wherever I wanted to go?'

'Yes, miss,' the driver responded.

'Well, I'd like to go home, but now the silly man wants me to have breakfast with him before I do. And after my unfortunate mugging last night I don't have a phone to call and tell him I can't. Can you take me to where he is, please?' she pleaded.

The driver started to frown.

Goldie hurriedly continued. 'It'd serve him right for me to just let you take me home, but I don't want to get into another fight with Gael. Not for another twenty-four hours, at least! So help a girl out—please?' She put on her best smile.

After the briefest hesitation, he nodded. 'Of course, miss. He's not too far away.'

'Thank you.' Goldie expelled a secret sigh of relief as he opened the back door and helped her in. The moment the door shut she unclenched her fists and closed her eyes as a deep shudder of unexpended adrenaline rushed through her.

The limo started to move and she was thrown back to last night. She should have walked away, found the nearest police station and taken her chances with the men in blue rather than the man in a black suit.

Pursing her lips, she squashed down might-have-beens and caught the driver's eye in the rearview mirror. 'Is he...is he in a meeting?'

Now she was doing this, the thought of an audience made her cringe—but not enough to alter her decision.

'Yes, miss. The production meeting should be done in half an hour.'

She fought back slight trepidation, nodded and murmured her thanks. Trying to calm her nerves was no use. Her heart was thrumming loud enough to block out the busy sounds of New York traffic as they traversed Midtown.

When the driver pulled up in front of a sheer glass office tower Goldie almost lost her nerve. The bundle of cash clutched in her fist—the representation of the grossest insult she'd ever suffered—spurred her on.

She exited the car and nodded her thanks.

The driver said, 'He's on the tenth floor, I believe. I've called the receptionist. She'll let you in. And, miss...?'

Goldie paused. 'Yes?'

'He probably deserves what's coming to him, but go easy on him.'

Her eyes widened. The tall, heavyset man, who might easily double as a bodyguard, doffed his cap with a discreet smile before getting back into the car. Bemused, she walked into the building, wondering why the driver was giving her access to confront his boss if he'd seen through her ruse.

Maybe he felt Gael deserved it? On account of having done it before?

Her bewilderment increased as the lift rushed to the tenth floor. But by the time she exited and was shown to the conference room her anger was firmly in place. She shoved open the double doors and entered.

Gael sat at the head of a large table, flanked by executives on either side. She didn't bother to stop and count how many people were in the room, but she knew all eyes had turned to train on her.

He saw her, froze mid-speech, his eyes widening, wary and watchful. On a screen to the side of him a vaguely familiar man also stopped talking and glanced her way.

'Goldie—'

'This is how you operate, is it?' She waved the envelope at him from the opposite end of the oval table. Her voice shook with anger, but she didn't care. 'What's the twenty-first-century version of *wham-bam, thank you, ma'am*? And, seriously, after *that* mind-blowing night I would've thought I'd warrant at least fifty thousand! Are you sure you don't want to revise the sum? After all, sleeping with a big, bad boss like you would gain me upwards of few *hundred* thousand if I should take it to the press, hmm?' she sliced at him.

He surged to his feet, planting his hands on top of the table as his cold eyes glared dire warning at her. 'Goldie, this isn't the time—'

'Or the place? I beg to differ. I think this is *exactly*

the time to show you what I can do. Isn't that what you asked for last night? For me to show you what I can do? And weren't your exact words something along the lines of, "*You're good. So very good*"? So what changed your mind between last night and this morning? I think I deserve to know that at the very least, don't you?'

His jaw clenched for one heart-stopping second. 'If you know what's good for you—'

She laughed—a bitter, spiky sound that didn't feel one little bit natural. 'What's *good* for me? I think we both know I made one gross misjudgement after another when I chose to trust a single word you said. I may be an actress, Gael, but you were very good at pretending too. Maybe you should try your hand at acting. But I need two small favours from you, if you'd be so kind?'

His jaw clenched. *'Sí?'* he said through gritted teeth.

'First of all, the next time you come across me being mugged, do me a favour and keep walking. I'm absolutely sure I don't need your brand of chivalry. And secondly...'

Darkened hazel eyes glared at her across the gleaming table. 'Yes?'

She ripped open the envelope, pinched the dollar bills between her fingers and flung the whole lot across the table. 'Take your sleazy money and shove it where the sun doesn't shine!'

Beneath the flying bills, stunned silence gripped the whole room. Gael's eyes blazed with incandescent rage.

Knowing she'd struck her mark, Goldie dramatically brushed her hands clean, then began to walk backwards, her eyes still connected with his, a triumphant smile curving her mouth. She'd clawed back some of her dignity. She might have cratered her career in the process, but that was a problem to be tackled another day. Her immediate problem for now was to find a way to get home. It looked as if she'd have to plough deeper into her meagre savings for a taxi ride after all—

The sound of applause froze her thoughts and her feet. Her mouth dropped open as more hands joined in with the clapping. On the screen, the man she now recognised as a famous director pumped his fist, his face split into a wide grin as he pointed an accusing finger at Gael.

'Gael, you sly, brilliant man! You spend twenty minutes laying into me for the delay to the production when all along you had *this* up your sleeve?' The man barked out another laugh, before turning his gaze to Goldie. 'You—Goldie Whoever-you-are—just made my day! I can already see the headlines…not that I court them of course. The media will lap you right up. Nothing captures the moviegoing public's imagination more than a newbie blowing their socks off. I don't think it's too premature to say welcome to the team—'

'Ethan, shut up for a moment,' Gael bit out, his gaze still locked on her.

He hadn't so much as moved a muscle since she'd flung his money in his face. And with each moment that passed she feared the look in his eyes would erupt into actual flames.

She'd made her point. She needed to get out of here. *Fast.* Despite the crazy talk spewing from the mouth of the award-winning director. Another step back brought her to the double doors.

'Come on. You trusted me with this project, Gael. Gave me carte blanche to find the best actress for the lead character. I know my broken leg hasn't helped matters, but—' he tipped his head towards Goldie, another smile splitting his face '—with this gem you've discovered we can start production almost immediately.'

Goldie frowned. 'I… What…? I don't know what you're talking—'

'Gentlemen, ladies—excuse me for a few minutes, *por favor*?' Gael interrupted once more.

He was rounding the table in quick, purposeful strides, his eyes cutting into her, silencing any further speech she could muster. Galvanised by the look in his eyes, she turned sharply, slammed her hands against the door in her rush to escape. When it opened she rushed through with fast, skin-saving strides towards the lift.

She'd poked the dragon in his den. Woken it. No need to stick around and watch the resulting inferno.

She reached the lift doors just as hands closed over her arms. Turned her firmly around.

Burnished eyes blazed down at her. 'You think you can create a spectacle like that and get away scot-free?' he seethed.

'It was nothing short of what you deserved,' she launched back, her hands going to the hands holding her prisoner in a bid to prise them off her. 'Let me go.'

He dragged her close and fired under his breath, 'Not until you're made to understand the consequences of what you did back there.'

'Whatever they are, they were worth it,' she returned defiantly.

A dark cloud descended on his face. 'Are you sure?'

'Yes, I'm one hundred per cent sure! Let me go, Gael.'

Behind her the lift door pinged open.

'Take a minute, Goldie. Think about what you're doing. Any hint that what you have just done *wasn't* an audacious audition could spell the end of your career. Are you prepared to take the risk?'

'To make my point that I'm not a whore you leave money on the bed for when you're done? *Absolutely.*'

His nostrils flared and a look passed through his eyes. Regret, maybe? Or surprise? She gritted her teeth.

'I don't think of you like that.'

'Oh, good—I'm so glad we've got that established. What about your note? You've "*decided to go a different route*"? The only difference between you actively pursuing me last night and leaving me that poor excuse of a *Dear Jane* note this morning is the fact that we slept together. So pardon me if my powers of deduction are right on point!'

His jaw visibly tightened. 'Calm down, Goldie.'

'No—and stop saying my name like that.'

'Like what?'

'Like I'm a recalcitrant child you're trying to manage. I'm done talking to you. I want nothing to do with you. Let me go and I'll try to forget we ever met.'

'*Santo cielo.* You should stop pursuing a career in acting and form an international debate team. You'd absolutely excel at it.'

Without waiting for an answer to his damning of her character, he dropped his hand from her arm to her wrist and dragged her towards another set of doors.

Shoving them open, he led her into an empty conference room, making sure to block her exit.

She didn't want to look at him—didn't want to be close enough to him to breathe in his unique scent, to watch the beauty of his square-jawed face and be reminded of how she'd explored his body last night, how he'd moved so powerfully inside her. So she stalked as far away from him as possible and stared out of the window at the Midtown traffic.

'Ignoring me isn't going to make this conversation conclude any faster,' he delivered.

She placed her hands on the window ledge to steady herself. She wanted to drop her forehead to the window too, but that would be one weak gesture too far. 'I told you, I have nothing further to say to you. Nor do I imagine you have anything to say to me. Your little note and the deplorable cash buy-off said it all for you. But I'm prepared to grant you two minutes. Say what you dragged me in here to say, then I'm leaving. And don't even *think* about trying to stop me.'

She sensed him prowling behind her for a full minute before he spoke. 'The money wasn't supposed to be taken the way you took it.'

What her laughter lacked in humour it more than made up for in scorn. 'Right. And I was born yesterday.'

'*Dios...*'

She heard his deep inhalation.

'I'm good at reading people, Goldie. Reading between the lines. Deny it all you want, but you're in a fix. Otherwise you wouldn't have fought for dear life to hang on to that tattered bag last night. And you wouldn't have chosen not to call a cab to take you home if you'd been able to afford it. Unemployment means different things to different people. I suspect in your case it means near destitution.'

Shame dredged her, sending prickles of tears to her eyes. She blinked it away rapidly. 'Bravo for that incisive dissection of my life.'

He sighed. 'Hate me all you want for pointing out the obvious. But you also mentioned that you needed a job quickly. The money was my gesture of assistance—'

Pride and anger made her whirl around. He was standing a few feet behind her. Tall and imposing and altogether too much for her roiling senses. 'I'm not a charity case!'

'No, you're not. And I didn't think you were.'

He paced a few steps before shoving his hands in his pockets. She was beginning to notice it was his self-calming gesture.

She supposed he needed calming after her calling him out and making a spectacle of him at his meeting.

'Are we done?'

He shook his head in a decisive movement. 'No, we're not done. You'll accept my apologies if I didn't make it clear that the money had nothing to do with what happened between us last night. It was a gesture of generosity, not payment for services rendered.'

A large dose of the hurt that lingered in her chest

abated, but she wasn't about to show her relief. 'Fine, apology accepted, but you can keep your money.'

She started to walk past him. One hand shot out of his pocket and slid over her hip. Goldie jerked out of the way, in no way wanting to be reminded of what it felt like to be in his arms.

'Please don't touch me.'

His jaw tightened but his hand balled and dropped back to his side. 'As you wish. But before you walk out the door and demolish the chance you've created for yourself, stop and think for a moment.'

'What do you mean, the chance I've created?'

One sardonic eyebrow went up. 'Are you really so blind that you can't see the bigger picture?' He stabbed a thumb in the direction of the adjacent conference room. 'In your burning need to make a point you've turned an unfortunate event into an opportunity. Are you going to cut off your nose to spite your face by walking away now?' He was almost taunting her.

She folded her arms. 'Whatever was going on in there is none of my business. If they've mistaken me for the actress you wanted to cast then you can explain their error to them. I'm leaving.'

He laughed. 'After going to all this effort to create a buzz for yourself?'

'Careful, there, or that apology you uttered a few minutes ago will seem like something out of a past lifetime and I'll resume detesting you.'

He shrugged. 'I state things as I see them. You came here to make a point. You've made it. Don't let the effort you've put in go to waste.'

'Are you seriously trying to tell me to capitalise on you treating me like a prostitute?'

A look crossed his face. 'Don't make this emotional, Goldie.'

'Wow. I'm sorry if I'm not as cut-throat as you.' She shook her head. 'Why are you even pursuing this? Your note was quite clear. You woke up this morning and decided you didn't want me after all.' She thought it best to ignore the telling gleam that reflected briefly in his eyes. 'So what's changed?'

The jaw already clenched tight hardened. Silence ticked by until she was sure he wouldn't answer.

Leave, her hammering heart urged. *Before things get any weirder.*

'Are you going to answer me, Gael?' she blurted.

Eyes raked her from head to toe before meeting hers full-on. 'You were a virgin. And you didn't think to tell me.'

Goldie swallowed. Fought the heat and trembling that had begun in her lower limbs. Suddenly she wished she'd stayed by the window, not been standing on her own two legs for this unexpected turn in the conversation. Thankfully, her legs held her up. And her chin rose when she commanded.

'I don't remember any instance during the night when we were obliged to exchange sexual histories. Perhaps you thought we'd be there all night while you recounted yours?'

The barb struck home, made his nostrils flare in pure Latin temper before he reined it in. 'Are you saying being divested of your innocence meant nothing to you?'

The harsh, condemning tone was back. But she wasn't about to stand for it any longer.

'What I choose to do with my virginity is my business. Tell me the experience was ruined for you because of it and I'll apologise.'

His eyes gleamed with pure carnal memory before he blinked, but that look singed her very skin.

'It wasn't ruined. Far from it,' he returned gutturally.

That blush she was fighting won the round. Heat surged into her face and she averted her gaze for a second. 'So what was the problem?'

'The problem is *why me*? Why now? Innocence at your age is rare. I can't help but draw certain conclusions.'

She stared at him, her brain firing wildly at her. It took a heartbeat or three for her to realise where he was coming from. Horror made her hand fly to her mouth. 'You think I hung on to my virgin status just in case a guy like you came along so I could hawk it for a huge payday?' Shock made her voice squeak.

He had the grace to look momentarily confused before his inscrutable expression returned. 'That scenario isn't a foreign concept and I'm sure you're aware of that.'

'I'm aware of no such thing! I'm not sure what circles you move in… Wait—scratch that. After my run-in with your conscience-free ex I can hazard a guess as to the depths your ilk are prepared to sink to for your sick pleasures. But think about this for a second. *If* I were that avaricious, don't you think I'd have negotiated my price *before* I slept with you?' she demanded.

He levelled a hard gaze at her, in no way swayed by her argument. 'That sort of innocence isn't always easy to prove before the event.'

Her mouth dropped open for several heartbeats before she managed to shake her head. 'My God, why…? How did you get like this?' she whispered, sheets of ice dredging her stomach at his blatant accusation.

His face closed completely and his every feature was devoid of emotion. 'I'm a bastard, *literally*—and, I'm told, figuratively. I've learned to accept that nothing that feels that good comes without a price.'

Goldie held her breath, unwilling to admit in any way that the newest emotion which had risen to join the riot of feelings inside her was sympathy for him. He was the bad guy here. He was the one causing her pain.

'Please take it from me that what I gave last night had no strings attached whatsoever. And then please let me go.'

Again a touch of confusion clouded his forehead. 'I don't think you understand why I brought you in here. Regardless of what I thought last night—and I'm prepared to concede that I may have got the wrong end of the stick with you—your performance in there has guaranteed you the part.'

There was zero pleasure in hearing that. She shook her head again. 'Why?'

'Because, believe it or not, that scene you just enacted is uncannily similar to one from the script. You weren't acting, but they thought you were. And you've won them over—especially my director.'

'Right. And you?'

He cast her an inscrutable look before he shrugged. 'What I think is no longer relevant. The only question now is, do you want the part or not?'

CHAPTER SEVEN

GOLDIE EYED HERSELF in the mirror as the make-up artist applied the final touches to her make-up. Her character, Elena Milton, was the same age as her, so there wasn't much to be done in the way of make-up for the early scenes—especially since the scene they were about to shoot was one that required her to be makeup-less.

The director, Ethan Ryland, was waiting for the sun to begin setting on the plains of the KwaZulu-Natal game park, where the next scene of *Soul's Triumph* was being shot.

In her hand she clutched the script, which she always kept close by even though she knew her part by heart and could recite every other part in the script too.

When the make-up artist pronounced her ready, Goldie jumped off the stool and headed outside. While most of the cast and crew chose to stay in the cool confines of their air-conditioned trailers and chalet when they weren't shooting, she preferred to absorb the stunning beauty of South Africa's south-eastern province every chance she got.

Probably because she still couldn't believe she was there.

The experience so far had been surreal, and Goldie couldn't believe they were already halfway to being done with the movie. She had certainly learned a lot in the last five weeks. And to think she'd never imagined she would be here at all...

After Gael had thrown his gauntlet at her feet that morning, just over a month ago, she'd spent a torn, frantic twenty-four hours weighing the pros and cons of accepting the less than wholesome opportunity he had dangled once again within reach.

At her mother's urging to do as much research as possible, she'd succumbed and looked up the man she'd given her virginity to on the internet. She'd come away stunned, albeit with a half-hearted understanding of why Gael Aguilar reacted with suspicion to everyone around him. The trait wasn't admirable by any stretch, and nor was it forgivable when it pertained to her. But it was clear that the sheer prestige and power he wielded along with his half-brother, Alejandro Aguilar, through their company, was enough to draw an army of sycophants and other unsavoury characters.

Even those who sacrificed their virginities in the hope of a pot of gold...

Whatever.

Had she believed in that sort of thing, Goldie would have toyed with the notion that destiny was hell-bent on giving her this role. Even after Ethan's repeated assurances that he was going to stop auditioning because he believed he'd found his actress she hadn't been convinced.

She didn't doubt for a second that Gael's involvement in the project was what had made her initially reticent about taking the part. Gael might have accepted that he'd got her motives wrong, but the hurt hadn't quite gone away. Probably because neither had the cynicism she glimpsed in his eyes whenever he looked at her.

It had only been after her second meeting with Ethan and his team—minus Gael—two days later that Goldie had started to entertain the idea that the opportunity *was* one she could grasp and launch a career out of.

Before that, though, there'd been her mother to contend with.

Gloria Beckett had been beyond ecstatic that her daughter had landed the plum role in a big production movie. But even as they'd celebrated with a trip to her mother's favourite restaurant, at Gloria's insistence, she'd worried about being absent from home for the long weeks shooting the movie would take.

She'd eventually divulged her worry to Ethan, only to find out Gael had lined up a list of sober companions for her to interview for her mother. Her mother had resisted at first, but once Goldie had made it a condition of her acceptance or rejection of the role Gloria had relented and let her hire Patience, the middle-aged companion.

In the week before she'd flown to Vancouver, where the other half of the film had been shot, Goldie had been able to rest easy when she'd seen how well Patience and Gloria got along.

Now, as she watched a family of elephants foraging, from the porch of the timber chalet which housed their on-location skeleton crew, she allowed herself a peaceful sigh and a small smile.

Ethan and the crew were a dream to work with. And as for the story...

She glanced down at the script of *Soul's Triumph*. The story of Elena Milton and Alfonso Veron was unbelievably powerful, at times disturbingly heartbreaking, but utterly sublime. A tale of triumph against adversity, it charted the lives of two unlikely souls each tied to a different destiny from the moment they met. But while common sense and inevitable heartache dictated they take different paths, they were continually drawn, for better or worse, back to each other, in an often shocking and volatile relationship that spanned decades and brought untold hardship to their families.

Today's shoot was the first meeting between Elena and Alfonso. Goldie had already met her Spanish lead, an actor in his mid-twenties who spoke very little English. Although he delivered his lines perfectly, conversation off-camera was minimal—a fact for which Goldie was secretly glad.

Even now, weeks later, she was still grappling with the tumultuous twelve hours she'd spent with Gael and wasn't in the mood to deal with much else, even friendly banter between co-actors. The crew for the most part also left her alone. Sure, they'd invited her along on their free day excursions, and she'd partaken of a few, and for dinner and drinks, of which she'd accepted none. She didn't think she would be able to accept a social invitation from anyone for a while after the Heidi debacle.

'Goldie, we're heading out in five minutes. You ready?'

She nodded and smiled, gave a thumbs-up to Ethan as he joined her on the porch. He returned the gesture with the tip of the crutch he still had to use, then turned to supervise the crew loading equipment into a Jeep in the car park.

Ten minutes later they set off, and Goldie found herself smiling again as the stunning landscape unfolded before her.

Ethan caught her smile. 'Is this your first time in Africa?' he asked.

'No, but it's my first to this part of Africa, and my first time when I know I'll keep a vivid recollection of it,' she answered.

He frowned. 'You've lost me.'

She laughed, although the sound was tinged with a deep-rooted sadness. 'I'm half-Ghanaian, but my last visit to my father's homeland was when I was a child. I don't remember much of it, and I haven't had a chance to visit since then, for various reasons.'

'Oh, right...' There was a note of sympathy in Ethan's voice but he didn't probe further, for which she was grateful.

They arrived at the location of the shoot and were greeted by the animal handler who would be keeping an eye on the cheetah needed for this scene. None of the animals in the private game reserve were tame, but one or two had been hand-reared due to injury. One in particular, a gorgeous, graceful cheetah named Asha, had won a part in the movie.

Goldie kept a respectful distance from the animal as she was readied. When she got her cue she made sure her running shoes were laced properly and waited for Ethan's signal.

Being chased by a semi-tame cheetah was in equal parts terrifying and exhilarating. Doing it three times, until Ethan was happy and before the sun dipped into the horizon, was a touch nerve-racking. But she managed it, and delivered her lines alongside the actor playing Alfonso, then smiled widely when she got a fist-pump of approval from Ethan.

'Scene Three is officially in the bag. Although I would *never* recommend getting chased by a wild animal in the savannah as a way to meet the love of your life for the first time.'

Amid the laughter and high fives for a job well done, Goldie looked up. And saw Gael lounging against the hood of the four-wheel drive furthest away from the cluster of crew vehicles.

Gael watched her eyes widen as she spotted him. Shock was swiftly replaced by deep wariness as she stared at him. The wide smile on her face from a moment ago faded to nothing.

He ignored the tiny spurt of regret that look elicited and shoved his hands into his pockets. It was only a matter of time before the rest of the cast and crew noted his presence. Gael had wanted a quiet moment before he was interrupted. He'd had his quiet moment, but he'd used it to question why he was here at all.

Sure, Alejandro and the Ishikawa brothers—his partners—had questioned him extensively on how the project was going, and he had promised them an update. But he could easily have video-conferenced with Ethan for a full report, as he'd done in the weeks since the project had got underway. He hadn't needed to fly for almost a day to inspect proceedings for himself.

But, hell, he was here now. And he didn't want to examine why, for the first time since he'd reached adulthood, he'd gone for a long stretch without taking a woman to his bed. He didn't want to examine why the only woman who seemed to stir his senses was the woman he'd shared a stunningly memorable night with. One who wanted nothing to do with him. One he knew deep in his gut he needed to stay away from.

And yet here he was...

He watched Goldie glance around her, as if she was debating whether to acknowledge or ignore his presence. Gael smiled to himself. *He'd* give himself a wide berth too if he could—especially after the few weeks he'd had.

It had started with his visit to Chicago three weeks ago, and Alejandro asking him to be his best man. It had gone downhill from there.

Every aspect of the Atlas Group's business was running like a well-oiled machine. And yet he couldn't focus—couldn't get past the thought that the past seemed to be on a collision course with his future:

namely in the form of the father he'd put out of his life
and his mind a very long time ago.

When, at the end of a fraught business meeting, Alejandro had suggested Gael return to his home base in
Silicon Valley to get his head straight he'd wholeheartedly agreed, jumped on his plane—and headed to South
Africa instead.

And now the woman who'd taken up more of his
thoughts than he was even marginally happy with was
trying to pretend he didn't exist.

The crew were beginning to pack up. Ethan spotted
him and waved, but Gael's cool nod as he approached
Goldie thankfully kept the other man away.

He reached her. Stared down at her. Her nostrils
quivered slightly as she stared boldly up at him. The
African sun had lent her skin an even more vibrant tone,
which made her stunning violet eyes more vivid and
alluring. Recalling how silky her skin was, how warm
and enthralling it had felt to touch her, he was glad his
hands were deep in his pockets. His senses were poised
on the edge as it was. He didn't want to add touching
where it wasn't wanted to his list of things to deal with.
But not touching didn't mean he couldn't look his fill.

His gaze raked the khaki-coloured dress she wore
with a tightly cinched belt that emphasised her small
waist, then her bare legs and the ankle boots adorning
her feet. She looked capable and utilitarian—as her part
demanded. But with the shoot over she'd let her hair
loose, and dark gold corkscrew curls bounced over her
shoulders. Again the memory of having his fist locked

in those waves tore through him, powerful and fierce. He clenched his gut against the sensation.

'It's good to see you, Goldie.'

'*Is* it?' She stopped, pursed her lips and shook her head. 'No. Sorry—I promised myself the next time I saw you I'd make an extra effort to be civil, so here goes.' She took a deep breath. 'Thank you for sorting out the sober companion for my mother. You didn't have to, but I really appreciate you doing that...so, thanks.'

He allowed the smile that tugged at his lips—the smile that had been nearly non-existent these last few weeks—to filter through. 'You're welcome. I wanted to give you peace of mind. I trust everything's going well in that department?'

She nodded, her eyes rising from where they had settled on his chest to meet his. She even deigned to offer a tiny smile. 'Yes, they're getting on like a house on fire, or so I'm told.'

'I'm glad to hear it.' He didn't want to begrudge her the peace of mind that was sorely lacking in his own life.

Her eyes searched his. Gael wasn't sure what she found, but her face lost a little of its tightness. He exhaled, realised he was breathing a little easier, and then turned when he sensed they were no longer alone.

Ethan approached on his crutches. 'The crew are about to head out, and the cast and I are heading for the airstrip. Goldie, do you want to join us? Or...?' he paused, his eyebrows lifted.

Gael shook his head. 'There's no need. I have my plane here. We can all fly back to Durban on my jet.' He nodded to Ethan's plaster cast. 'I'm sure you'll be much more comfortable on my plane than on the turboprop.'

Ethan laughed. 'Now, there's an offer I'm not about to refuse. We'll meet you at the plane?'

Gael nodded. Waited until his director hobbled off before he turned to find Goldie regarding him with a steady look.

'Without inciting an argument, can I ask why you're here?' she asked.

He shrugged. 'My partners wanted an update. So did I. And Durban is great at this time of year, I'm told.'

'So you're here on a working vacation?' she probed.

The inkling that he wasn't wanted deepened a pang he didn't want to acknowledge. About to tell her he hadn't taken a vacation in a decade and wasn't about to take one now, Gael paused. 'Why not? I've been told I'm "grumpy and insufferable" lately. So maybe a time-out is just what I need.'

That minuscule smile reappeared. 'Did whoever dared to make that observation get away with their lives?' she teased, and fell into step beside him as he headed for the last remaining vehicle left in the deserted dirt car park of the game reserve.

'Sadly I had to rule out homicide. Doing away with my future sister-in-law before she becomes my brother's wife—or even at any time after that—will *not* end well for me. My only choice was to remove my grumpiness from her presence.'

Her smile widened, turned into a laugh.

Something twitched in Gael's chest at the sound—

a feeling of wanting to join in, to revel in her warm amusement at his own expense.

Her cute nose wrinkled when he stopped beside the truck and stared at him. 'So you're here to foist your grumpiness on us instead?'

He opened the door and saw her into the passenger seat. Shutting the door, he leaned an elbow on the open window. 'I'm in the land of cheetahs, fireflies and stunning sunsets, amongst a thousand other pleasures. I'm certain I'll find a useful outlet for my mood,' he murmured.

The sparkle in her eyes didn't dim, but her amusement altered as a different sensation arced between them. Gael recognised it. Waited for her to recognise it too. He didn't exactly plan on doing anything about it—she'd made her feelings abundantly clear that day in his conference room—but the moment felt too visceral to dismiss. So he stood there, with her breathtaking face and body mere inches away, and watched her eyes darken as sexual awareness zapped the air between them.

Abruptly, she averted her gaze from his. 'Can we go, please?'

'Of course,' he murmured.

Despite his intimation otherwise, he *was* here solely on business. Although in hindsight he accepted that he might have handled their morning-after differently, he stood by his decision to keep his hands off Goldie Beckett.

For one thing, she was now effectively his employee— and mixing business with pleasure never boded well in the long run. His brother and Elise might have proved the exception to the rule, but statistics weren't in favour of such occurrences ending well.

For another, he hadn't forgotten what he'd witnessed in that auditorium at Othello. Her virginity might have proved that she hadn't gone through with the director's proposal, but Gael had seen her allow the director's touch. Had seen her take the keycard, watched her consider the proposal. As much as he wanted to explain that away, he couldn't.

Especially as since then Goldie had as much as admitted that her career was her top priority. That she would do anything to further it. Who knows what would have happened had Gael not come along? Hell, her immediate reaction to being drunk for the first time in her life had been to enquire whether her actions had affected the opportunity he'd been offering her.

On some level Gael admired her dedication, and it was undeniable that she had the talent to back the ambition. But the thought of her doing *whatever it took* left a bitter taste in his mouth, reminding him too much of the issues he was dealing with when it came to his mother. Rightly or wrongly, he couldn't think of one without thinking of the other. They both struck a little too close to home and, despite her attempting to explain herself to the contrary, he hadn't been able to erase Goldie's last performance with that director in the auditorium from his mind.

As a tool for enabling him to keep his hands off her it was effective, he mused as he slid behind the wheel and turned on the ignition.

The ride to the private airstrip where his plane was parked was conducted in silence, and took less than ten minutes.

On the plane, he let Goldie wander off to take a seat next to Ethan. As much as it struck an unpleasant chord within Gael, he ignored the feeling and struck up a conversation with the actor playing Alfonso, who was glad to connect with a fellow Spaniard, even though Gael only half paid attention to their discourse.

His gaze was drawn inexorably to the woman chatting in low tones to Ethan. Her occasional husky laugh bounced across the space between them and sizzled along Gael's nerve-endings.

He was almost relieved when the plane landed in Durban forty minutes later. This time an appointed driver chauffeured them to Umhlanga and the Oyster Box Hotel, where the cast and crew were staying. After agreeing to have a proper meeting with Ethan the next morning, he trailed after the departing Goldie. She was standing in front of the private lift that served his suite when he joined her.

Her eyes landed on him and widened. 'You're staying in the presidential suite too?'

'According to the bookings manager it's the only suite with a spare bedroom not already taken up by the cast and crew. I hope you don't mind sharing?'

A frown clenched her forehead for a few seconds, before a resolute look slid across her face. 'Of course not. She mentioned that the other room might be used by other people. I just didn't think...'

'That I would be your first room-mate?' he finished.

She eyed him a touch warily as he stepped into the lift beside her. 'Yes. But it's not a problem. The bedrooms are on different floors, so hopefully I won't disturb you too much.'

Her smile was less natural than it had been on their ride back from the game reserve. Gael experienced another bite of regret.

'I will let you know if I'm planning any wild parties.'

This conversation was ridiculous. He wanted her at ease, but he was aware that he himself wasn't at ease. So he let silence rule for the remainder of the short lift journey and their walk to the entrance into the suite.

'Have dinner with me,' he invited.

The offer had been delivered without much forethought when she'd started to beat a hasty retreat towards the stairs that led to the suite upstairs.

She paused. Her sumptuous lips parted. 'I don't think…'

'In the interest of fresh starts and civil leaf-turning, I also wish to make an attempt. You haven't eaten yet, have you?'

Gael wasn't bothered by the knowledge that he was pushing. He was known for remaining civil with the women he'd had liaisons with—Heidi being the only exception—so why not Goldie?

Slowly, she shook her head. 'No, I haven't.'

He nodded, a welling of satisfaction moving through him. 'Do you want to eat out or in?'

'I had planned on taking a shower, then ordering in…'

He crossed to the dining room and returned with a

lavish menu, which he held out to her. 'Decide what you want and I'll have it delivered here for us by the time you're done with your shower.'

He saw a look of refusal cross her face before whatever resolution she was striving to achieve forced a nod from her.

'Okay.' She took the menu and scanned it quickly. 'I'll have the lobster bisque to start, the chicken *involtini* and the lemon cheesecake, please.'

He took the menu from her with a wry smile. 'Nothing local for you? I can recommend something if you prefer?'

She grimaced. 'I tried a selection of dishes a couple of nights ago. They were heavenly, but sadly they didn't agree with me.' She rubbed a hand across her midriff. 'Turns out my constitution isn't as adventurous as my spirit.'

Gael frowned, his gaze following her hand. 'Are you okay?'

'Yes, I'm fine now,' she replied. 'But I think I'll stick to food that I know for now. I'll see you in half an hour?'

He nodded, watched her shapely legs stride up the stairs and then resolutely turned away. They were being civil, sharing a suite like reasonable room-mates—not two people who'd shared a sizzling, passionate few hours in bed a few short weeks ago.

So he *wouldn't* imagine her undressing, stepping into the shower, rubbing shower gel all over her incredibly responsive body...

A low curse flamed from his lips. The libido that hadn't so much as twitched around any other woman he'd come into contact with since he'd slept with Goldie was now threatening to rage out of control.

He crossed to the phone and relayed their dinner order. Then he went into his own room and showered.

She was back downstairs when he emerged, wearing a flowing *boubou* gown in a distinct African print, with her hair brushed loose and wavy. The bold oranges and reds complemented her dark colouring, making her look even more striking.

His gaze travelled from her exquisite face and down her body. When she caught his eyes on her bare feet, she grimaced and wrinkled her toes.

'I hope you don't mind? My feet have been in hot and sweaty boots all day. I can't bear the thought of confining them again.'

For some absurd reason he couldn't pull his attention from her peach-painted toenails, nor stop himself from stepping closer to breathe in the unique scent he was sure didn't come out of a tube of luxury product. Goldie's scent was one he hadn't been able to get out of his mind.

'Of course not,' he replied, his voice curiously gruff.

Her smile dragged his eyes up. Gael found himself absorbing it, wanting to bask in it. To perpetuate it long into the night.

Dios, what was wrong with him?

'Would you like a drink?' he asked abruptly.

Her smile dimmed.

Do better. He needed to do better. As much as he enjoyed sparring with an argumentative Goldie, he admitted he liked this 'new leaf' version better. She still had the fire he was drawn to, but in this place and time he could almost forget that there was a facet of her character he quietly despised. It was a naked ambition she was willing to do just about anything to achieve, and he knew he wouldn't be able to abide it into the future.

The future? What future?

He had no plans of reinitiating or prolonging anything.

He'd built an empire.

He'd dated beautiful women.

And he'd vowed never to marry any of them because, inevitably, each and every one of them showed their true gold-digging and opportunistic characters eventually.

On top of that he had known from an early age that he would never produce a child who might feel a trace of the sting of rejection he'd suffered.

Nothing would change that particular vow. Not even Alejandro's engagement and the subtle hints about revisiting old ground that he kept tossing Gael's way. That, most of all, was a grenade he intended to keep tossing back into his brother's lap.

'An apple spritzer?' he tried again, careful to keep his voice even.

Her nod was a touch wary. 'Yes, thank you.'

Although there was a drinks console nearby, Gael crossed the room to the well-stocked bar, to give himself—and her—time to adjust, regroup.

He heard her pad over to the large rectangular windows that opened onto the wide patio and the stunning view of the Indian Ocean beyond. After fixing her drink he poured a glass of burgundy for himself and joined her outside, where the table had been laid by the private butler.

They sipped their drinks and watched the rolling waves hit the shore on the beach down below for a few minutes before their food arrived.

Halfway through their first course she raised her gaze from her plate. 'How long are you planning to stay?' she asked in an even voice, but he detected the thin nerves behind it.

'Until I can no longer avoid my duties as my brother's best man.'

Her eyes widened. 'Your brother's getting married that soon?'

'In ten days,' he answered, aware that the tension he'd hoped to dispel was still very much present.

'Why is it that he's getting married but you're the one who has the jitters?' she asked, and her acuity was a touch disturbing.

'I wish him well, of course, but the inescapable truth is that a lifelong commitment like marriage more often than not fails eventually.'

She frowned. 'You think your brother's marriage is going to fail?'

He shrugged. 'We don't come from admirable stock when it comes to the sanctity of marriage. He's…brave to want to give it a try, nevertheless.'

Troubled violet eyes connected with his. 'I… What you said back in New York about being—'

'A bastard?' His jaw clenched. He thought about evading the suddenly abrading question, thought about how they'd ended up here in the first place. 'I'm the product of an affair my mother had with Alejandro's *still married* father.'

Her mouth dropped open. 'Oh.'

He took a large sip of wine. '*Sí*. Oh.'

She shook her head. 'I didn't mean *oh* like that. I mean, I'm the last person who should be shocked...' She stopped and frowned. 'If Alejandro's asked you to be his best man, then your relationship with him must be good—so your past circumstances can't matter that much to him?'

Gael recalled their last fraught meeting. Recognised that this time all the tension had been his alone. Although Alejandro had resisted at first, lately he'd been much more open—most likely thanks to the influence of his fiancée, who was open-hearted and open-armed about embracing new family, seeing as her own family situation was lacking.

'The relationship isn't without its challenges, but it's...progressive.'

'So it's progressive now, but you think that relationship will fail too?' she pressed.

He frowned. 'There are always adverse factors at play.'

'And you intend to take those adverse factors lying down, just like you do with your businesses?' she asked lightly as she cut into a piece of chicken.

'I have never failed at a business venture,' he quipped.

'So why are you prepared to write off a sound relationship and watch it fail without putting in as much effort as you would into a business venture?' she parried.

His smile felt as cynical as his soul. 'Because business is conducted and thrives without the single detrimental component that damns us all.'

'And what's that?'

'Useless emotion.'

Her fork stilled and her eyes widened. 'You think emotions are useless?'

'They're more harmful than useless. They cloud judgement and ruin lives.'

Gael knew he'd been unable to hold back the bitterness ravaging him when her face clouded with something close to sympathy.

Goldie shook her head. 'How do you...? I don't understand.'

He gritted his teeth, tried to stem the words that seemed determined to spill. And failed. 'You recall your little story about infidelity and alcoholism?'

'Of course,' she said.

'The former has been the story of my life—what my building blocks are based on. I left Seville over ten years ago and thought I was free of it. Turns out I'm not.'

'Your mother?' she queried cautiously.

A vice tightened around his chest. 'And Alejandro's married father. Version two point zero.'

Anxiety darted across her face at his tone. Her fingers toyed with her water glass before she asked, 'Does Alejandro know? Does his mother know?'

He laughed harshly. 'Alejandro knows. He seems to have found a way to accept it, but I haven't been so fortunate. As for his mother—yes, she knows. Most likely she enjoys the chaos associated with it. They all seem to thrive on it, in fact.'

Enlightenment whispered over her face. 'That's what you were talking about that night? What you meant when you referred to—?'

'Toxic relationships? *Si, Goldie mia*. When it comes to those types of relationships I am vastly knowledgeable.'

Her expressive eyes shadowed. 'I'm so sorry.'

Gael frowned, wondering why those two words sank deep inside him, attempted to soothe a place he'd believed was too mauled by past pain to be still alive. The sensation was so alien it robbed him of breath and speech.

Thankfully the butler arrived with their dessert course. Gael refused the sweet platter in favour of an espresso, hoping the caffeine would clear his head and put a stay on his runaway tongue.

Goldie's cheesecake was set before her with a flourish that drew a small smile from her. He nodded his thanks when his drink was handed to him.

About to gulp down the hot beverage, he looked up, frowning, as Goldie turned green.

She bolted from the table before he could utter a single word. Gael rushed after her—only to hear the bathroom door slam shut before the sound of violent retching sounded from within.

His gut tightened in alarm. 'Goldie?'

More retching, followed by a low, miserable moan. He knocked on the door, turned the handle. It was locked.

'Open the door, Goldie.'

A grunt filled with discomfort, then a cough. 'Um… no, I'm fine. I'll be out in a second.'

He gritted his teeth. 'You're not fine. You're vomiting.'

He absently wondered why that observation filled him with alarm, why the helplessness assailing him grew with each futile second.

A half-laugh sounded. 'Yeah, I think I'm aware of that little fact—' Speech ended and retching restarted.

He resisted the urge to ball his fist and pound the door open. '*Dios*, why did you lock the damned door?'

No answer. More vomiting.

He had to satisfy himself with waiting for her to finish emptying the contents of her stomach before she answered.

'Because I didn't want you to see me.'

'Modesty is the last thing you should be concerned about if you're sick. Can you open the door—*por favor*?' He tried his most reasonable voice.

'No. I… I'm feeling better. I'll be out in a minute.'

Argumentative Goldie was back. Short of breaking down the door, Gael could only grit his teeth and resign himself to pacing the hallway until he heard the sound of the lavatory flushing and a running tap.

When she didn't emerge for another five minutes his anxiety swelled higher. 'Damn it. Open the door!'

'Sir? Can I help with anything?' The solicitous butler had appeared behind him.

Gael curbed the urge to demand the spare keys to the bathroom, accepting that perhaps he was overreacting. Goldie had mentioned having a stomach upset after some food two days ago. He could still hear movement and the occasional splash of water, so she hadn't passed out—or worse.

'No, we're fine. If I need anything I'll call.'

He waited until the butler had left, then returned to the bathroom door. 'You have two minutes to come out, *guapa*. Then I'm coming in.'

'Okay, fine.'

He hesitated for a second, then returned to the patio. He poured a glass of water and downed it, then poured one for her in case she needed it.

He knew less than a minute had passed, so he forced himself to the balustrade to stare unseeingly at the view. He *was* overreacting. Goldie being sick might disrupt the movie's shoot, but it wasn't something they couldn't overcome.

But if it was more than a stomach bug…if she was falling ill with something else…

When his practised deep breathing barely calmed his flailing control, he cursed under his breath.

'Gael?'

He whirled away from the view, his relief at seeing her standing there more welcome than he knew it should be. Her hair looked tumbled and a touch wild, as if she'd run her hand through it several times without a single care about the way she looked—which put her firmly in a unique category far from most of the women he'd dated.

Framed in the light spilling from the living room, she was a gorgeous sight, despite the paleness of her face. A sight he wanted to see more of. Much more, he realised. And accepted. Perhaps he'd been too hasty to consign them to being just temporary room-mates. The chemistry between them was beyond electric. It was unique enough to warrant further investigation. Exploration of the best, carnal kind.

Prising himself off the low wall, he walked towards her. Saw the mixture of horror and acute trepidation in her eyes. And froze.

'Goldie! What's wrong? Do I need to call a doctor?' he demanded, his voice turning harsh with barely curbed concern.

'No, I don't think so.'

'You don't *think* so?'

'I… I think I know…' She stopped and swallowed, then a charged little tremble shook her frame. 'Gael, I think I'm pregnant.'

CHAPTER EIGHT

THE LIFE-CHANGING WORDS uttered out loud locked something deep into place inside her. Goldie had no explanation for it, but she knew she wouldn't need a pregnancy testing kit or a blood test to confirm the truth burning in her heart.

She was pregnant.

From her single night in Gael Aguilar's bed she'd fallen pregnant.

And he…he looked as if he'd been hit by a giant wrecking ball.

She turned around, stumbled back into the living room, sank down onto the sofa. Despite the juggernaut of emotions tumbling through her she heard him approach, take up residence in front of her. A glance upwards showed him with crossed arms, the skin around his mouth pinched tight as eyes turned dark and turbulent pierced her.

'You're pregnant.'

The words were devoid of emotion. But they demanded confirmation.

'You don't just *think*? You're sure?' he grated out in an icily controlled voice.

She licked dry lips, went over the dates she'd spent the last ten minutes in the bathroom desperately calculating. When they fell a good fourteen days short—*again*—she nodded.

'I'm late. I'm never late. I just thought… God, I don't know *what* I thought. I know it sounds naive, but I thought having sex and…and getting ready for this job may have disturbed my cycle.' She met his gaze, saw the frigid disbelief there and closed her eyes. 'Trust me, I know how that sounds. But with everything that's happened these past few weeks…' She stopped and stared at him. 'Are you going to stand there glaring at me all night?' Her voice shook, and, oh, how she hated herself for it.

'What else is there to say? Except maybe congratulations?'

Her stomach threatened to roll again. She placed a soothing hand over it. 'I don't know about that. I haven't taken it in yet.'

'*Haven't* you?'

His voice was a stiletto, cutting through the noise in her head.

She glanced up, and her heart dropped to her feet at the look on his face. 'What are you implying, Gael? What exactly do you mean by *congratulations*? On the pregnancy or on something else?'

'You need clarification?'

'Yes!' She surged to her feet, swayed, and sat down again. 'Please don't tell me you think I did this *deliberately*?'

Light, cold eyes stared unflinchingly back at her.

'Perhaps not the failure of the condom, but I'm afraid the "naive" argument doesn't fly. You're an intelligent woman, Goldie. I don't believe you ignored your hitherto *regular* cycle at all. You knew you were pregnant but chose not to say anything.'

'Why would I *do* that? Why would I be so—?'

'Calculating? I can think of a few reasons.'

Horror clenched her heart in a vice. 'Enlighten me, then, please.' Her hands began to tremble with the force of her chagrin and the shock that was rocking through her. She curled them into her lap and fought the prickle of tears that burned her eyes.

'You're already on the fast track to stardom—thanks to a few well-placed circumstances. But this pregnancy guarantees you the fastest possible route to achieve your aims.'

'My *aims*?' she whispered.

'You want to be a successful actress, do you not?'

She shook her head in confusion. 'Yes, of course I do—the same way you strive to be successful at what *you* do. I love what I do and I'm good at it. But I've also worked hard for it. There's nothing wrong with that and I won't apologise for it.'

'Of course not. Just as there's nothing wrong with the few hundred thousand starlets who want the same thing you do. Except you saw an opportunity for a fast track and you took it.'

'An opportunity *you* told me I'd be a fool to refuse, if I remember... Oh, you're still talking about the pregnancy? You think—' She stopped, too horrified to put what she suspected he meant into words immediately.

He raised a mocking eyebrow, dared her to continue.

'You think that just because you own a production company I deliberately kept this a secret, so I'd be set career-wise and security-wise for life?'

'*Sí*. Exactly.'

She shook her head again, unable to fathom how he could read her so wrong. How could he be so twisted about her motives? Or complete lack thereof. Had his past circumstances really done such a damaging number on him that he truly believed that?

'Gael, let me make one thing clear. I didn't want to lose the opportunity you presented me with, once you yourself talked me into it. But, please believe me, I would never put my career before the welfare of an innocent child,' she stated, her heart dredged with a hurt whose depths she couldn't quite touch.

'Sadly I have no proof of that besides the words falling from your mouth. *Will* have no proof of that until the child is born,' he rasped icily.

'How…? What did I do to make you think this of me? We barely know each other—'

'I know enough.'

'To condemn me like this?' she rasped, feeling her voice, like everything inside her, threatening to go numb at the flaying condemnation she saw in his eyes.

'On the way back from that dinner party in New York did you not plead with me? Tell me that you'd do *anything* to get the part?'

'Anything within reason. Like an audition. Or a screen test. Even an initial interview to see if my credentials were what you needed. Something *within* my profession. Not…not *this*!'

His eyes followed the hand she slid low over her stomach, then his gaze rose to hers, icier, more soul-shredding than before.

'*This?* The baby is a mere *thing* to you?'

'Oh, please—why are you trying so hard to twist my every word?' she cried, blinking back the further tears that threatened. 'I didn't trick you, or keep this baby a secret from you. I've only just worked it out myself. I'm not out to get my hands on your billions, or use the baby as leverage for my career. I haven't even been able to absorb the news and you're already labelling me a heartless gold-digger who would trade her unborn child for fame and fortune!'

'You wouldn't be the first,' he drawled, the same way he had that day in New York.'

Pain, raw and bracing, ripped through her. 'You know what? Go to hell, Gael. And stay there!'

This time when she stood her feet felt more inclined to support her.

He took one step forward.

She countered by taking several away from him.

He halted. 'Where do you think you're going?' he demanded, his voice quiet but grating.

'Anywhere I don't have to continue this ludicrous, demeaning conversation with you. I'm not one of the women you've dated in the past who came with a port-folio of agendas. Hell, we're not even dating. So leave me alone.'

'Goldie—'

'No! If you have something else to say to me that *doesn't* involve you shredding my character, talk to me in the morning. Otherwise I'll thank you to stay away from me.'

He laughed. 'Stay away from you? When you're carrying my child? Believe me when I say that will not happen in a million years. We *will* talk in the morning, Goldie, whether you wish to hear what I have to say or not.'

'Don't count on it.'

'Goldie—'

'Goodnight. I'd say sleep well, but I hope you spend the rest of the night thinking about your unfounded accusations and stewing over them.'

Her words, his warning—*everything* rang in her ears long after she'd brushed her teeth and slipped between the covers.

The shocking reality that history had well and truly repeated itself for another Beckett was so visceral it brought tears to her eyes. Goldie herself was the product of a one-night stand, conceived when her mother had been part of a charity's volunteer group in Ghana and had fallen for the charms of a local businessman. But, unlike the men who'd followed, her father had tried to make it work, even moving continents to be with her mother.

Sadly, her mother had been unwilling to settle for being a wife and mother in a picket-fenced house. Gloria had believed there were bigger and better things out there for her. Her reluctance to give their relationship a chance had eventually driven her father back to his homeland, leaving her mother to fall prey to dreams that had never been fulfilled and a lifetime of being taken advantage of by unscrupulous men.

Goldie had always known in her heart that the lessons she'd learnt via her mother's experience wouldn't lead her down the same path. But one night's wrong decision *had* led her here. Only this time she was the one being called unscrupulous. Avaricious.

She hated the tears that welled up in her eyes. Hated Gael in that moment for making her feel lower than she already felt. Because what had they created together other than a child who would hate her, and possibly its father too, for bringing it into a world where there was no chance of its parents ever being together?

Goldie knew how lonely and frightening things could get. Already she feared for her child. In light of Gael's revelations about how he felt about his family, how could she not?

Her hand slid over her stomach as weariness and inevitability washed over her in equal measures. She didn't have all the answers for how she was going to deal with what was happening to her. Far from it. But Goldie knew without a doubt that she would fight to her very last breath to make sure her child didn't suffer an ounce of preventable pain or rejection. Just as she knew that if that involved battling with Gael Aguilar she would bring the same fervour to the task.

With that resolution burning bright in her chest, she closed her eyes and willed healing sleep.

Her sleep was relatively peaceful. But twice she got up in the night to throw up. Twice she heard Gael prowling through the suite. Clearly her curse had worked, but she couldn't take any joy in that. She shut her mind to it, concentrated only on making it to the bathroom and back to bed both times.

It was almost as if now her mind had caught up with what was happening in her body her baby was determined to make its presence felt one way or another.

She fell asleep just before dawn, her hand on her stomach, her mind whirling with a million thoughts.

Less than an hour later she was up. Determined to stick to some sort of routine, she donned the aqua-coloured bikini she'd used since coming to Durban, and threw a light matching sarong over it. Slipping her feet into gaily coloured sandals, she settled a wide-brimmed hat on her head and drew back the sliding doors to step out onto the private patio fronting her bedroom. Steps led down to the beach and the dramatic shoreline.

Pausing to breathe in the fresh air, she let her gaze drift past the iconic red and white Umhlanga lighthouse to the gleaming waters of the Indian Ocean. Seagulls flew overhead in the early-morning sun, and Goldie blanked her mind as she struck out for the quarter-mile walk along the shoreline.

Pregnant. She was *pregnant*.

She would buy a pregnancy test to confirm it as soon as she could, but even without the visual proof with each pulse of the word in her brain her breath caught. She reached the end of her walk and stopped to face the ocean, her mind spinning.

How would a child fit into her world? Where would

they live? *How* would they live? How would her mother feel about being a grandmother?

How did Gael feel about being a father?

That question stood out above all the myriad hurtling through her head. It was also a question whose answer she knew she'd discover soon.

Swallowing, she raised her face to the warming sun's rays for a minute, before shedding the sarong, hat and sandals and walking into the sea.

Swimming was blissful, as usual, but already she worried about what such active exercise would do to her baby, and gave up halfway through her normal lengthy swim. Collecting her things, she strolled back towards the side of the hotel. The first thing she needed to do, once she'd had a talk with Gael, was to dig up as much information as she could on how to keep healthy during pregnancy.

Once again she was assailed with a frightening but growing thrill over her impending future.

No matter what. She'd fight to her last breath.

Discarding her things on a lounger next to the private pool that served the presidential suite, she turned on the outside shower to wash off the salt water. She was washing sand from between her toes when she heard the hurried slap of bare feet.

'Where the hell have you been?' Gael demanded forcefully. 'I was about to send out a damned search party.'

She turned, her gaze momentarily obscured by the water running down her face. Sluicing it away, she tilted her head back from the spray. He was livid, the chest beneath his white polo shirt rising and falling as if he'd run a marathon.

'I went for a walk on the beach, followed by a swim,' she said, fighting to keep her voice on an even keel. She needed to keep calm. For her baby's sake.

'Without bothering to tell me?'

'I went for a swim yesterday too. In fact I've walked and swum every day since I got here. I do it before breakfast and before we go on location. Should I have reported to you then too?'

Fury blazed across his face as he stepped closer. 'Don't be flippant, Goldie. You know what I mean.'

'Do I? A few things have changed, granted, but are you seriously expecting me to turn my life upside down because—?'

His hand slashing through the air chopped off her words.

'*Everything* has changed, Goldie. Accept that now, before we exchange further words.'

About to contradict him, she stopped. Because he was right. *So* right.

For one thing, once their child was born this man who stood brimming with fury and power before her would be connected with her for ever. And if he chose to take an interest—and judging by the look on his face he already was—he would have a say in her child's welfare.

The thought sent a shiver through her. Weirdly, it wasn't a shiver of terror. More a dread of the unknown. Because suddenly another factor loomed large in her brain. This child wasn't hers and hers alone. It also belonged to Gael Aguilar.

The thought was unsettling enough to make her words tumble out. 'Gael... I... It was just a walk. A swim.'

'And what if something had happened to you?' he rasped.

'The beach is safe. Nothing would have happened.'

He gritted his teeth for a few tense seconds, before his gaze flicked to the torrent of water cascading down her body. 'Are you done?'

She nodded and turned off the shower. 'Yes.'

Glancing round, he spotted a pile of towels and grabbed the largest one. Goldie reached up to smooth back her wet hair, then froze when she caught his eyes on her.

Slowly, Gael advanced, his hot scrutiny rushing down her body and returning on a slower trajectory. 'How could you not have known you were pregnant?' he scythed in a heated voice barely above a guttural whisper.

Her breath knotted in her lungs. 'Excuse me?'

Light hazel eyes reached her breasts, lingered for a long moment. 'Your body is already changing. How do you expect me to believe you didn't know?'

'There was so much going on. I... I wasn't paying attention. Gael, I didn't know—I swear.'

His mouth tightened, but he handed over the towel without acknowledging her words. 'Come inside when you're done here. We need to have that talk.'

She watched him walk away, his strong, shorts-clad

legs taking him from her view in seconds. She took her time to dab the excess moisture from her body, even though it didn't buy her any more time to formulate her thoughts.

Simple reason was, she had no idea what was coming with regard to Gael.

When she walked into the living room he was pacing, the phone pressed to his ear. He stopped, his gaze fixated on her as he spoke. 'Work it out, Ethan, and let me know.'

The hairs on her nape prickled as she watched him hang up and toss the phone onto the dining table. 'What was that about?'

He gave a tight, mirthless smile. 'Setting out contingencies.'

'What does that mean?'

He prowled to where she stood. Scrutinised her face and body one more time. 'First things first, *guapa*. How do you feel?'

The question was solicitous, caring. The emotions bristling from his body and eyes told a different story.

She sidestepped. 'Why are you asking?'

'You were up during the night. I have a doctor on standby—'

'I don't need a doctor. I feel fine.'

A tic manifested at his temple. 'You found out you're pregnant last night. Don't you want to know immediately how best to take care of yourself?'

She frowned, knowing she'd walked into that. 'I... Of course.'

He nodded, and strolled back to the table. Grabbing

a white paper bag, he handed it to her. 'Before the doctor comes let's make absolutely sure of your state, shall we?'

Still frowning, she took the bag, looked inside. 'A pregnancy test...' She wasn't sure why the band tightened around her chest. She'd planned on getting one anyway. But Gael doing so seemed...*hurtful*.

'We need to be equipped with as much information as possible going forward, do we not?'

The explanation dissolved a little of her hurt, but not all of it she noted as she nodded and headed for the bathroom.

Gael was standing at the wide rectangular windows staring out at the view when she emerged from the bathroom. He turned immediately when she walked into the room, his narrowed eyes piercing hers before dropping to the two sticks clutched in her fist. Quick strides forward brought him unapologetically into her personal space.

'Well?' he breathed, his eyes gleaming with a feverish look.

Goldie swallowed. 'Yes.' She handed him both sticks.

He stared down at the tests, his gaze riveted on the writing displayed on the tiny screen.

Pregnant. 3+ Weeks

After an age, he tossed both tests onto the console table behind her. Closing the gap between them, he speared his fingers into her hair, angled her head up so she couldn't look away from him.

'You're carrying my child.'

The primal claim in those four words was unmistakable.

Her breath shook as she nodded.

The palms cupping her cheeks firmed, as if he was focusing her attention ready for his next words. He pulled her close until their faces were inches from each other's.

'Do you accept that this fundamentally changes your life, Goldie?'

The depth of his belief in the words almost shook her enough to frighten her. But she'd worked too hard for the life she'd chiselled out for herself to cower beneath anyone's will.

'No, I don't. I'm sorry, Gael, but it doesn't.'

CHAPTER NINE

IT DOESN'T.

For a few seconds Gael was sure he'd misheard. Then he remembered exactly who he was dealing with. A woman with an iron will almost as strong as his own.

The woman carrying his child.

Surprisingly, his senses had stopped reeling somewhere in the middle of the night—between Goldie's first and second vomiting sessions. The test he'd procured first thing, when he'd thought she was still sleeping had merely been the instrument to slide that last one per cent of doubt from red to green.

The one and only time a woman had tried to trick him into fatherhood before, her quest had been tentative and ultimately bungled. Heidi had hinted at pregnancy towards the end of their time together—most likely to test the waters and her chances in the marital stakes. Gael's firm shut-down had resulted in a firm retraction of her fictional state.

Not so with Goldie. Her conviction had been firm, which in turn had cemented his.

She was carrying his child.

He was going to be a father.

But she didn't think it was a life-changing situation for her. What did *that* mean?

'*Perdón?*' Realising he'd lapsed into his mother tongue, he shook his head. 'What do you mean, *it doesn't*?'

She licked her lower lip, triggering a wave of heat through his groin. Nothing that had happened in the last twelve hours had changed the red-hot chemistry between them. If anything, the changes in her body had lent her skin a deeper glow, made her even more voluptuous and unbelievably stunning and heightened the awareness between them. A fact his body was reacting to in the most primal way.

'I mean *some* things will change, of course. I'm not debating that. But I'm not changing who I am because of my baby.'

His fingers wanted to tighten, to draw a more satisfactory answer straight from her mind. He cautioned himself to relax, breathe deep. '*Some* things? Tell me what you think those things are. Then tell me what you think *won't* change.'

Her mouth firmed for a second. 'I haven't laid it all out in a spreadsheet, if that's what you mean—'

'But clearly you've given it some thought, Goldie. So let's have it. Bullet-point the big things for me.'

She exhaled. 'Well, the first thing is to make sure the baby is healthy.'

'*Sí*—agreed,' he said.

'Then, once he or she is born, we'll have to discuss

your visitation rights and how to work around our career schedules.'

His gut tightened, disbelief flashing through his system. 'Visitation rights? *Schedules?*'

She nodded.

He dropped his hands and fought the terrible rush of dark fury and the memories of being discarded when it suited his mother that surged high. 'And where will you be living while these rights are being discussed?'

She frowned, as if his question was absurd. 'In New Jersey, with my mother—hopefully in a place that better suits us.'

'Of course. So I'm to remain in California, where I'm based, only seeing my child when a court order stipulates, hmm? Presumably you intend to pursue your career?'

'I…yes.'

'So our child will be left in the care of minders, or your mother and her sober companion, perhaps, while you're off on location around the world? Or do you intend to drag him or her with you?'

Her violet eyes grew wide, probably at his seemingly calm tone. 'Gael, I told you I don't have all the answers yet—'

'That is exactly right. You do *not*. But I do. Before I tell you, though, I have a little tale to tell you. Are you ready to hear it?'

She blinked, then raised an eyebrow. 'Do I have a choice? Aren't you going to tell me anyway, whether I want to hear it or not?'

Gael took another step back—because right in that

moment he wasn't sure whether he yearned to kiss her sensual lips in an attempt to force down the memories surging, or condemn her for making those volatile emotions rise to the fore in the first place.

She shifted in reaction to the invisible fireworks sparking round the room, drawing his attention to her body, barely covered by the wispy sarong.

He whirled, slashing his fingers through his hair, and tried to seek a little clarity from the wide expanse of the ocean beyond the window. When it remained elusive, he took a deep breath and turned around again. Facing this thing head-on was the only viable option.

'I've told you a little bit about my past...my parentage, *si*?'

'Yes...' she responded warily, her gaze tracking him as he began to pace.

'What you *don't* know is that every few years when I was growing up my father would leave his wife for a few weeks and convince my mother to go away with him. Every time it was supposed to be *the* time—the moment when he left Alejandro's mother and made a life with my mother, the woman he supposedly truly loved. At those times I was parcelled off to the local orphanage or left with casual acquaintances who were paid to mind me.'

She inhaled sharply. 'Gael—'

He held up his hand. 'I'm not telling you this to gain sympathy. This is a fact of my childhood. It's behind me now, but it's not forgotten. I have accepted that I didn't even have a broken home to call my own—that my day-to-day existence was at the whim of a father who confirmed explicitly that I was an unwanted mistake when I dared to confront him.'

She gasped, her hand flying to mouth as if to cover the sound, the pain.

'I have had no interest in becoming a father simply because it's not a role I ever foresaw for myself.'

'But—'

'But now I am faced with the prospect of bringing my child into the world, things are not as clear-cut. However, there is one thing I intend to ensure will *never* happen where this child is concerned.'

She stared, unblinking, the pulse in her throat hammering wildly. 'Wh-what is that?'

'Comparing the circumstances I've just described to you with what you proposed a short while ago, do you think a man in my position, and with my power, having gone through what I went through as child, will be willing to stand idly by while my child is shuffled between minders, planes, movie locations and court-ordered visitation rights?' he gritted out.

Her mouth trembled for a second before she caught hold of herself. 'Gael, please be reasonable—'

He broke off mid-pace and planted himself firmly in front of her. He needed her to see the intent emblazoned in his heart and mind.

'Let me answer for you, Goldie. The scenario you propose will happen *over my dead body.*'

The words sank in.

Her mouth dropped open in disbelief. 'So we're not even going to discuss it?'

'We just have.'

'No, we didn't. You're just trying to lay down the law.'

'I have told you what I intend *not* to happen with my child. We can now go on to discuss what *will*.'

'*Our* child.'

'What?'

'*Our* child. Equal parenting. Equal responsibility.'

'Yes—agreed. And that most definitely does *not* involve split homes on either side of the continent.'

'You can't just rule things out, Gael. We need to agree a compromise.'

'Why compromise when I have the solution?' he asked.

Her smooth forehead clenched in a frown. 'We confirmed the pregnancy less than ten minutes ago. How can you have a solution already?'

'Very easily when what's at stake is this important.'

She gave a slight shake of her head, but her gaze didn't leave his. She blinked, her expression turning wary with trepidation. 'I think we need to talk about this some more.'

'I'm finished with talking, Goldie. The soundest solution to the situation we find ourselves in is for you to marry me.'

Even though her senses had screamed at her that whatever Gael was about to propose would most likely push all her alarm buttons, the words still hit Goldie square in the chest with shocking and relentless force.

She swayed on her feet.

Gael cursed, caught her by the elbow and tugged her to the sofa. 'Sit down, Goldie.'

'I'm fine.'

'I didn't say you weren't. I would still like you to sit. You were up half the night, throwing up, and you've been standing for far too long.'

She rolled her eyes, earning herself a dark frown. 'Women have been giving birth for thousands of years without turning into wilting flowers for the duration of their pregnancy, Gael.'

'*Si*, but none of them have had the privilege of carrying my child,' he bit out.

Her mouth quirked in a parody of a smile, which vanished a second later. 'Do you have *any* idea how pompous that sounds?'

'You ask the question as if I care. You're still standing, Goldie.'

She plunked herself on a seat. Then rubbed her temple as his words attacked her once more. 'You just… You just asked me…'

'To marry me, yes,' he confirmed, his voice brimming with unequivocal power and certainty.

'But…why?'

'Because my child won't be living in New Jersey. It will be living with me.'

Cold dredged through her. 'And the only way I will have access to our baby is to marry you? Is that what you're threatening me with?'

He didn't answer immediately. Silence ticked by as he paced in front of her. Then he stopped and propped his hands on his lean hips.

'Tell me a little bit about your background, Goldie.'

Her gaze flicked up to meet his. 'Why?'

'Because I want to understand why you're fighting this, when all signs indicate that you would think this a perfect solution if other factors weren't an issue. So make me understand why our child can't be with *us*, full-time, wherever that may be.'

'I don't have to *make* you understand. Just because you suddenly think marriage is a perfect solution, when only last night you were dead against it for your own brother, it doesn't mean I agree.'

'I don't think it's a perfect solution. I think it's the most viable one.'

She batted the answer away. 'I would really like not to talk about our child as if it's a commodity you're brokering.'

His head went back as if she'd struck him. 'Trust me, *pequeña*, a commodity is the last label I'd hang on our child.'

The words were soft but deadly. Too late, she remembered what his parents had done to him as a child. Gael might deny it, but that period in his life had left scars. Deep scars that still dictated his motives.

'Sorry,' she muttered. 'I didn't mean to… It's just that you speak CEO all the time.'

He lifted one eyebrow. '*All* the time?'

A fiery blush flashed into her cheeks at the blatant reference to their night together. Recollection surged into her mind, making her breath shorten. Unable to drag her gaze from his, she watched, fascinated, as his eyes turned dark and stormy. Despite the brightness of the room she suddenly felt as if they were cocooned in a dark, decadent piece of heaven.

Which was absolutely the last thing she needed to be thinking about now.

He seemed to arrive at the same conclusion. He blinked and gritted his jaw. 'I'm all ears, Goldie. You grew up in a broken home, correct?'

She winced. 'Eventually, yes.'

'And your father? Is he in the picture?'

'Long-distance.'

He pursed his lips. 'Given the choice, is that what you *wanted* to happen when you were growing up?'

She closed her eyes. Swallowed. 'Okay, you've made your point, but I still think we can make an alternative arrangement—'

'No.'

She glared at him. 'Let's explore another option. Couples live together full-time without marrying. Why do we need to be married?'

'You don't think our child's conception from a one-night affair is more than enough for it to have to deal with? You want to add to the long line of illegitimacy in his history? When you can prevent it? What have you got against marriage?'

'I… Nothing. But that doesn't mean I want to be knee-jerked into it.'

'The welfare of our child should be nothing like a knee-jerk response. It should be *everything* to you.'

Her mouth dried at the enormity of what he was saying. While she'd been lost in dreamless sleep, it was clear Gael had spent hours thinking about the situation they found themselves in. He had a brilliant mind, but she didn't think he'd put together this presentation on the fly.

Still, what he was suggesting was so…*absolute*.

'Speak up, Goldie. What's the problem?'

She laughed, unable to believe he was expecting an immediate answer from her on so monumental a subject. '*If* I decide to do this, I want a few stipulations of my own.'

His brow clamped in a frown. Then he gave a tight nod. 'Let's hear it.'

'You…you can't want to be saddled with me for the rest of our lives, nor I with you, so can we agree to a more temporary solution?'

He froze. 'You want to enter marriage with a clause that ends it on a particular date?'

'Please don't make it sound so clinical. Until ten minutes ago you were a man who didn't date the same woman for longer than six weeks! Now you expect me to believe you're willing to give up the rest of your life?'

'For the right reason—why not?'

The right reason. The baby. Not them.

'I think you're missing the point, Gael. You automatically assume that putting a ring on my finger will make this baby's life stable. I'm not denying it will, but don't you think he or she will be happier with parents who are content?'

'Are you saying marrying me sentences you to a life of discontent?'

'Don't put words in my mouth. I just want us to take a step back, think about this—'

'Five years.'

'I... What?'

'You want a fixed term? We'll give it a try for five years. After that we'll reassess the marriage. Whatever the outcome then, one thing will remain non-negotiable. We'll live in the same city and do everything to provide a smooth home-life for our child. So—five years. Do you think you can give up your independence for that long?' he bit out.

'Gael—'

'And in that time, provided you make our child's happiness your number one priority, you will receive ten million dollars per year and five guaranteed box office smash movie roles courtesy of Atlas. You say your career is important to you? This way you can rest assured it will not be unduly interrupted.'

Shock held Goldie rigid for so long she wondered whether she was in danger of turning into a fossil. When she managed to speak again, her voice shook with effort. 'And...and if I don't agree to what you're suggesting?'

Goldie was almost afraid to ask, because the purpose she'd sensed in him when he'd confronted her outside seemed to have magnified a thousandfold. She didn't need to be a genius to work out that Gael had just given her the 'either' scenario. There was a very big 'or' coming her way.

'If you don't agree, then I'll take steps to remove our child from you—completely—the moment he or she is born. I'm sorry, *amante*, this is too important for me to beat round the bush. So those are your only options. What's it going to be, Goldie? Yes or no?'

* * *

Two days.

She'd argued for time to think about Gael's proposal. He'd grudgingly given her the remainder of their time in South Africa.

So she had two days to come up with a different solution, one that *didn't* involve marrying a man she barely knew, or fighting him in court for custody of their child. And so far, a day later and with twenty-four hours' worth of filming a beach scene between Elena and Alfonso completed, she'd drawn a blank.

To fight Gael she needed far deeper pockets than she currently had. This was her first movie role, and the pay was more than she'd dreamed of, but it was nowhere near enough to take care of her child while fighting for its rights in a court of law—especially against a powerful man like Gael Aguilar. And part of her contract with Atlas involved exclusive work that might extend for almost half a year after filming, which meant that even if she wanted to be pounding the pavements on job-hunts while being heavily pregnant she couldn't.

Which brought her to the option Gael preferred. Marriage.

Her heart caught every time she thought of that, but after a few times Goldie admitted that the idea wasn't as stomach-clenching as it had first seemed.

Both their backgrounds had proved conclusively that coming from a broken home could damage a child. For the longest time Goldie had felt bitterness and anger towards her mother for not being strong enough, for pushing her father away and breaking up their family. And, although she loved and supported her mother now, she couldn't help but feel bruised inside from the times when she'd lived in constant fear that her mother would never be strong enough to make the right decisions about the men she'd let emotionally abuse her.

In her darkest moments, Goldie had wondered whether she was potentially equally fallible. It was one of the reasons why she'd hung on to her virginity for so long. She'd been afraid to find out the depths of her strengths and weaknesses.

She didn't plan on being alone for the rest of her life. And did she not owe it to her child to try and give it the best possible start in life? Even if it meant marriage, temporarily, to its father?

She didn't know everything there was to know about Gael, but he'd laid the cards that were important to him on the table. The most commendable of which involved making their child's wellbeing his number one priority. Despite the flipside being his threat to fight her for custody of their child, her rational and emotional sides felt satisfied that he was committed to his unborn child.

Enough to decide to turn his private life upside down for it within hours of finding out about its existence.

That quiet but powerful truth made her turn her head now to look at the man in question, who sat next to her as the helicopter flying them to Table Mountain soared over the breathtaking landscape.

The crew had left Umhlanga early this morning. Because of tourism restrictions, they had only a small window to shoot a scene on the mountain—which, ironically, was the scene in which Elena was proposed to by Alfonso. A scene which ended with her saying yes, and then spending the rest of her fictional life fighting to save her marriage.

Dread whispered over her skin. As if he sensed her inner battle, Gael turned narrowed hazel eyes on her. He watched her silently for a few seconds before he reached across the bench seat to take her hand.

The action was unexpected, throwing her thoughts and emotions further into conflict. Provided she kept their child as their main focus, *could* they make a go of a five-year emotionless marriage? Because she wasn't about to delude herself into thinking there were any emotions involved here. Gael was acting purely on a primal instinct to protect what was his. Much as he would in a business venture.

Whereas she…

Goldie stopped her chaotic thoughts as the helicopter landed. She honestly didn't know *what* she felt. All she knew was the pledge she'd made to protect her child.

So, although she didn't attempt to remove her hand from Gael's once they alighted and were seen into the cable car that would take them to the top of the mountain, she turned her thoughts to work and the scene in front of her.

The view from the top was unlike anything Goldie had ever seen. Enough to rob her of breath for a full minute. Enough to make her feel like a small cog in the great, unrelenting circle of life. Enough to lend her the gravity she needed to utter her lines in a way that saw the scene completed in one continuous take and Ethan give yet another pleased fist-pump the moment he yelled, *'Cut!'* But while the crew celebrated she moved off to a quiet corner of the section of the plateau, her thoughts turning inward as she drank in the spectacular view of Cape Town and the ocean beyond.

She sensed Gael before his body heat arrived behind her. Strong arms bared to the African sun came around either side of her to rest on the railing.

'Do you really need another day to think about this, *cara*? You know deep inside what needs to be done, Goldie,' he rasped in her ear.

'Do I?'

'*Sí*, you do. Don't drag this out unnecessarily.'

'I don't want to. But…*marriage*…'

He moved closer, his body caging her in tighter. She angled her head, looked up at him. Eagle-sharp eyes stared down at her, their focus unwavering.

'Don't overthink it or confuse the issue. We're not fictional characters. We can have a marriage without the melodramatic chaos.'

She gave a tiny anxiety-filled laugh. 'How can you be so certain?'

'Because we don't believe in the fairy tale. We're going into this with our eyes wide open. There is only one purpose here. We're doing this for the sake of our child. For the chance to give it the stability we were both denied. Say yes, Goldie. You stand to gain far more than you stand to lose.'

His voice was hard, almost merciless.

She swallowed hard. Slid her hands over her flat stomach, her thoughts churning.

Gael's hand sliding over hers, warming her hands,

cradling their child, alarmed her almost as much as it settled her. He was claiming. But he was also protecting.

She would deal with the former if it threatened her at any point. The latter, she couldn't fault.

Taking a deep breath, affirming her pledge, she gave her answer. 'Yes.'

CHAPTER TEN

THEY LANDED IN SPAIN three days later. Once she'd given her answer things had moved at lightning speed. Papers had been drawn up, witnessed and signed, granting her unimaginable wealth and the type of acting roles that should have made her ecstatic but instead had left a faintly bitter taste in her mouth.

Somewhere along the line Gael had managed to weave her into agreeing to attend his brother's wedding. If she recalled correctly, his answer when she'd expressed reservations at attending had been a tightly voiced, 'You're about to become my wife. Who else am I supposed to go with?'

The suggestion that perhaps he might go alone had been met with a frown and a firm refusal.

'You will have to meet my family, as dysfunctional as they are, at some point. Best to get it over and done with. Besides, for once I would like to enjoy an event without Kenzo Ishikawa getting on my case about my marital status.'

'Kenzo Ishikawa…one of your business partners?'

He'd snorted, his jaw going tight before he'd replied.

'He seems to take pleasure in pointing out that I'm less of a man because I'm unattached. Our first attempt at a merger fell apart partly because of it.'

'And this is your chance to rub your attachment in his face?' Goldie hadn't been sure whether to be offended or amused. She'd chosen to be neither.

But Gael had sent her a tight smile. 'Exactly so. There is also the added bonus of beating Andro in the nuptials stakes, even if only by a few days,' he'd added with surprising relish, before absenting himself from her presence.

Now Goldie rose from the lounger and padded to the edge of the Olympic-sized pool.

Before that wedding happened there was the small matter of *her* wedding. Special licences had been arranged. Ethan had agreed to shoot a few of the scenes that didn't involve her, then give the whole cast and crew a four-day break before they resumed filming again at the end of next week. And Gael was having her mother and Patience flown over tomorrow, for the wedding that would take place here on his estate just outside Barcelona.

The place was quintessential Spanish architecture at its best. A rambling two-storey villa, the property sat in the middle of acres of rich green valley dotted with orange and lemon trees. The villa itself, originally a Catalan manor house, modernised and extended, was made of stone, with grand arches and a vast courtyard decorated with trellises and carefully groomed vines. The house was stunning and yet homely—a place she wouldn't have immediately associated with Gael Aguilar, the ruthless and ambitious CEO who wrote computer code as a hobby.

But then a few things were beginning to surprise her about Gael—not least being this marriage he was hell-bent on in order to protect his unborn child.

In the last twenty-four hours private doctors had visited her, taken blood samples and delivered enough pre-natal advice and vitamins to stun a horse. It was too early for an ultrasound scan, but Gael had readily agreed to a suggestion to listen to the baby's heartbeat on a foetal Doppler. The loud sound echoing through the guest bedroom where she slept had brought a look of almost shocking determination to his face.

It was that determination that strengthened her belief that she was doing the right thing too.

So when Gael's housekeeper walked out a few minutes later, to announce the arrival of the stylists and the gown designer contracted to ready her for her wedding, she took a deep breath, turned around and headed for her destiny.

Goldie climbed the small hill towards the tiny chapel that sat half a mile from the villa. A tiny part of her was glad for her mother's fussing around her, because it took her mind off what was waiting for her beneath the ancient steeple. She also knew it was her mother's way of accepting what was happening.

Despite Goldie's reassurances that she was doing the right thing, her mother had voiced her worry from the moment she'd landed. Eventually she'd accepted

Goldie's assurances, but it hadn't taken away the veil of concern in her mother's eyes.

Goldie's worry as to whether that concern might trigger a deeper reaction in her mother had been allayed by Patience, and the companion's brief but buoying report of her mother's progress had settled Goldie's own anxiety.

So she let her mother fuss now, because it meant *she* didn't have to do any fussing. She hadn't seen Gael in the past twenty-four hours—a surprising turn-up since she hadn't expected him to observe tradition. In his absence, questions had loomed—one in particular taking up most of her thoughts.

It was the question of sex—horrifyingly triggered by her mother's observation of the vast amounts of bedrooms in Gael's villa and how she was looking forward to seeing it filled with grandchildren.

Of course that had also brought on the question of how much of their agreement they would be sharing with others.

All those questions beat hard like butterflies' wings in her belly as she reached the doorway of the chapel. Technically, her mother was to walk her down the aisle, but Gloria wanted to walk a step behind, her hoarse insistence that this was Goldie's day, not to be spoiled by a mother who'd let her down, having brought tears to her eyes.

There'd been no time to utter words of comfort, or to take in her mother's new, more hopeful outlook on life, but something had settled in Goldie's heart upon seeing her mother again. For now, though, she needed to head up the aisle and join her life with Gael Aguilar's.

The man in question turned his tall, imperious frame and speared her with a fierce, possessive look as she walked slowly up the aisle.

He was impeccably dressed in a dark navy suit and snow-white shirt, his hair tamed and gleaming beneath the dozens of candles glowing from the cast-iron holders that hung from the ceiling, and his magnificence seriously threatened her breathing.

As his gaze raked her body she derived quiet satisfaction from the fact that she'd chosen a dress she loved, which gave her a much needed boost of confidence. The short-sleeved, cream silk lace gown that framed her figure to end in a short train behind her prohibited long strides. She'd forgone a veil in favour of a tiny tiara that held her pinned up hair in place. She wore only light make-up, and simple pearl earrings belonging to her mother adorned her ears to complete the subtly elegant ensemble.

Halfway to the altar, with her eyesight better adjusted from the almost blinding sunlight to the candlelit interior, she caught a better glimpse of Gael's face. And her breath caught.

Beneath the possessiveness, that hard look she'd never been able to fathom lurked in his eyes. A feeling of having been tried and found guilty for a crime she had no inkling of committing assailed her, causing her to stumble slightly.

She stopped to right her footing. Gael's nostrils flared as he took in her hesitation. Goldie started to shake her head, but he was already striding down the aisle.

Catching her hand firmly in his, he escorted her up

to the altar. Murmurs went up in the small wedding party comprising her mother, Patience, Teresa—his housekeeper—and her husband, and the driver/bodyguard who gave her a small smile as she passed him.

They had barely stopped before the priest when Gael nodded at the tall, thin man to proceed.

The bilingual ceremony passed in a blurred rush from one moment to the next.

Her mother stepped forward to relieve Goldie of the small bouquet clutched in her fist. Then Goldie was listening to Gael's deep, firm tones as he said his vows. Her eyes widened when his driver stepped forward with two rings laid out on a small velvet pillow. Gael's was a simple broad gold band, hers a platinum double circle with yellow diamond studs holding the two rings together.

Her fingers shook as she held his ring poised over his knuckle and repeated her own vows. A furtive glance at Gael showed his complete attention on her as she uttered the binding words. When she had finished an unfathomable look crossed his face.

In that moment Goldie was certain she'd crossed a threshold she would never be able to step back from.

Gael had experienced a well of satisfaction as he slid the wedding band onto her finger and repeated the words that had made Goldie Beckett his wife. He'd secured his child's future. Ensured it would never suffer the stings of illegitimacy and rejection he'd suffered. Would never be made to feel like an obstacle or an unwanted possession, either through emotional neglect or in the face of its mother's ambition.

He forced aside the rush of bitterness that stormed him. So far he'd been able to keep his feelings under control—had been able to contain the knowledge that Goldie's *yes* had come after his offer of compensation and a promise of a flourishing career.

He wanted to keep his emotions out of it—much as he kept his emotions out of his business transactions. And yet the boulder that had lodged itself in his chest since her acceptance of his deal wouldn't shift.

It shouldn't matter. Ultimately, he'd done what needed to be done for the sake of his child.

And yet it did matter.

He knew it mattered when he was invited to kiss his bride and sealed his mouth to hers and felt her brief hesitancy before her response kicked in.

It mattered when her gaze wouldn't meet his as they acknowledged the applause and smiles of their small group of guests once the ceremony was officially over.

He had married her to secure his child's wellbeing.

So why did his own suddenly feel precarious?

'Gael?'

He shut off his thoughts and glanced at his bride. They'd returned home from the chapel to an alfresco lunch set up on a banquet-like bench beneath two orange trees in his garden. He'd invited the rest of his staff to join them, and had endured the endless toasts with an ever-stiffening smile.

'Yes?' he responded.

'Are you okay?'

His mouth twisted. 'Of course. What could possibly be wrong on a day like this?'

She frowned. 'Please don't patronise me. Have I done something wrong?'

His jaw gritted. 'Goldie—'

'You've barely said two words to me since we left the church. In fact we've barely had a conversation since we arrived here. I know we're only doing this for the baby—'

'I would prefer it if you *don't* share our private agreement with the world.'

'That's just it. Why are we pretending to everyone that this is some sort of...love-match?' she demanded in a hushed tone.

'For the same reason we are entering into the marriage. To protect our child.'

'But...'

'Enough, Goldie. If you want to discuss this further we will—but not right now, *si*?'

Another member of staff—the head of Gael's vast stables—rose just then, to make a speech, effectively stopping her from speaking. Then there followed more speeches, mostly in Spanish, which meant she was left in the dark as to what was being said. But raucous laughter gave her a general hint.

She ate selectively, having eventually worked out which foods triggered her nausea and which would mostly likely stay down.

At one point, she caught her mother's speculative gaze swinging from her to Gael and back again. Although Goldie smiled, she wasn't sure it had been convincing enough.

She waited until Gael was occupied with entertaining a couple she'd been told were vintners from two estates away before excusing herself and returning to the villa. Accompanied by a smiling Teresa, who had insisted it was tradition that she help her dress for her wedding night, and her mother, who continued to cast curious glances at her, Goldie was forced to keep the starchy smile pinned on her face.

The moment Teresa departed, her mother faced her.

'You're pregnant, aren't you?' Gloria declared, her gaze running searchingly over her daughter's negligee-and-dressing-gown-clad body.

Her damning blush was all the confirmation her mother needed.

'Oh, Goldie…' The words were softly spoken, partly in regret, partly in tearful acceptance.

'I was going to tell you when the time was right.'

Her mother nodded, but her eyes remained troubled. 'Is that why you married him so quickly?'

It's why I married him at all. But she knew she couldn't say that. 'It's the right thing to do, Mom.'

'For you or the baby?'

For some reason that softly voiced question tightened a vice around her heart. She watched her mother's eyes fill with tears again as she sank down onto the bed. 'This is my fault. I'm so sorry, Goldie.'

She shook her head. 'No, it's not. Stop crying, please.'

Her mother's smile was sad and a touch weary. 'You can stop trying to be the adult, here, sweetheart. I know I haven't been the best role model for you. If I'd tried to make a better life for you, instead of selfishly wanting things I couldn't have, you wouldn't have rushed into this—'

'I made the decision with my eyes wide open, Mom. I… I don't regret it.'

She firmed her voice against the tiny white lie. The truth was that things had seemed so clear-cut on top of Table Mountain when Gael had whispered in her ear that this was the only viable option. But as she'd made her vows in that ancient chapel there'd been a terrible moment when she'd tried to imagine saying another set of vows, at another time and place, to someone else. The stunning realisation had come that she couldn't imagine such a time, couldn't picture another man. That she wanted this time and place to be the only occasion when she said those words.

Goldie still hadn't been able to wrap her mind around that.

'Are you sure, sweetheart? Because—'

'I'm sure, Mom.' She placed her hands over her mother's and held her gaze, repeating the words to herself in the hope that they would begin to ring true.

Her mother nodded and rose. Thinking she was about to head for the door, Goldie's breath caught when her mother wrapped her in a firm embrace, laying her cheek on top of Goldie's head.

'I should've done better. I should've been a better mother, fought harder to make us happy. I'm sorry, Goldie. I hope you forgive me some day.'

Tears filled her eyes, choking her response. 'Mom…'

'Shh, it's okay, honey. You'll do much better than me—I know you will. But if you ever need me please give me the chance to be there for you, okay?'

Unable to speak, Goldie nodded, then sat in silence as her mother left. She was still perched on the bed when a knock came on the door to the adjoining master suite.

The door opened to reveal Gael, minus his jacket and tie. He prowled into the room, power and glory falling from his impressive frame. 'Should I take it as a personal affront that my bride deserts me before the wedding banquet is over?' he drawled.

Her insides tightened. 'We're alone now, Gael. You can drop the pretence.'

He kept coming, not stopping until he reached the bottom of the bed, where he leaned his long-legged frame against the post, crossed his ankles. 'Where is the pretence, *amante*? You *are* my bride, and I *did* feel deserted.'

'So what is this? A yearning to have my fawning act reprised behind closed doors?'

His eyes narrowed as he stiffened. 'Act?'

'You don't wish anyone else to know this marriage is a sham, but do *we* have to pretend that there's more to this union than there really is?'

'Correct me if I'm wrong, but isn't this our wedding night?' he demanded bluntly.

Alarm and more than a touch of breathlessness stabbed her. 'In theory, I guess…'

His harsh laugh made her wince. 'No, Goldie, not in theory. In *fact*.'

Her stomach flipped. 'What are you implying?'

His mouth twisted. 'You were a virgin the last time we were together, but surely you don't need me to draw you a picture of what happens on the night following a wedding?'

She flushed, but boldly met his gaze. 'Of course not. Except I'm certain that picture doesn't apply to us.'

He slowly straightened, his chest rising and falling in measured breathing as he closed the gap between them. Goldie willed herself to stay still and not bolt the way her senses were screaming at her to.

'Explain to me how you arrived at this interesting conclusion?' he invited, his tone deceptively casual.

The dark gleam in his eyes said he was very much interested in her answer. And that it had better be to his liking. Or else.

She licked suddenly dry lips and searched for clarifying words. 'We're doing this for the baby, aren't we? And sex…sex will just cloud the issue. Blur the lines.'

He gave a hard, short laugh. 'So let me get this straight. You're perfectly content to condemn yourself to a nunlike existence for the next five years, and presumably you expect me to willingly subject myself to the same sexless fate?' he asked, his voice reflecting how ludicrous the idea was.

Goldie opened her mouth, shut it, then shook her head, confusion and exasperation filling her. 'This is why I wanted more time before we jumped into marriage. These are things we should've discussed beforehand—'

'So we could waste hours or days arguing it to death before you saw reason and gave in?'

Hurt and anger firmed her mouth. 'I'm not a shrew, Gael. I'd thank you not to make me out as one.'

'Very well. Tell me in simple terms that your assumption is ridiculous and we can progress with our wedding night.'

'There isn't going to *be* a wedding night! We have a deal. Sex isn't part of it.'

His nostrils flared and his eyes blazed with quiet fury. 'Only because I didn't think I needed to spell out so obvious and fundamental a point.'

'I'm sorry it's such an important thing for you. It's not to me.'

He rocked back on his heels, his features freezing like ice. 'I see. You get what *you* want out of the deal and to hell with the rest—is that it?'

'What are you talking about? I said yes because we both wanted—'

His hand slashed through the air. 'Save it, *cara*. We both know that fifty million dollars and a guaranteed five box office hit movies had a big hand in you eventually saying yes.'

Raw ice doused her. *'What did you say?'*

'Your hearing is perfect, Goldie,' he drawled. 'And I'm finished with talking.'

Her mouth was still gaping open when he took the last step and untied the belt of her dressing gown. The silk slid off her shoulders without much effort, leaving her in an emerald-green negligee.

Before Goldie could protest, one firm hand slid over her nape. He pushed her back onto the bed and prowled over her to plant his knees on either side of her hips. In the next instant his mouth plunged, hot and heavy and demanding, over hers, his tongue stabbing between her lips to take and ravage hers.

Her shock dissipated under the flames of his arrogant, unstinting caress. Despite a large part of her brain reeling under the accusation he'd flung at her, she couldn't help but moan when one hand boldly cupped her engorged, sensitive breast. Her breasts seemed to have grown a size bigger almost overnight, their tips super-sensitive as pregnancy hormones ran riot through her. Gael was clearly appreciative of her new size, and his moans grew more guttural as impatient fingers brushed aside the straps and yanked the top part of the negligee down her arms.

He broke the kiss to stare down at her full breasts. Eyes firing a burnished gold, he took the globes in his palms and toyed mercilessly with the nerve-engorged peaks.

Her head went back as she arched under the exquisite assault. Goldie knew she shouldn't be enjoying herself this much, that what he'd said to her needed to be addressed immediately, but the sensations zinging through her body, arrowing demandingly between her thighs, were too thrilling to stop.

She cried out as his mouth closed over one stiff nipple. Several expert flicks had her hips twitching, her breath shooting out in shameless pants as liquid heat ploughed through her. Back and forth he alternated his attention between the stiff peaks. Sent her right to the edge of bliss.

And then it *did* stop.

The loss of sensation was so acute she whimpered.

The sound shamed her even as she launched her fingers up to stay him, and eyes she didn't remember shutting flew open.

'Gael…?'

'*This* is why I didn't think I needed to point things out to you. The chemistry between us is as natural and vital as breathing. But if you need to be told, then hear this. Unspoken or not, sex *is* part of the deal. You may have a ring on your finger, but—trust me—this isn't a point I'm prepared to concede. So argue with yourself all you want to as long as you come back with a yes. Because tomorrow night the only bed you'll be sleeping in is mine.'

He stepped off the bed with the grace of a jungle cat and stood for a moment, staring down at her.

Words stumbled through her dazed senses—begging, pleading words that had no shame under the heavy weight of her thwarted need. With super-human effort Goldie bit them back. He'd dealt her the gravest of insults, attacked her integrity. Even if she risked expiring from the gut-clenching desire clamouring through her she wouldn't give in. Not when she knew his true feelings towards her.

Raising her chin, she firmed her mouth and returned his stare in silence.

Gael's mouth twisted with mocking bitterness. Leaning down, he traced a forefinger from her clavicle to her cleavage. 'That's how it is to be, hmm? Well…good luck, *cara*,' he murmured in a soft, deadly voice.

Then, turning on his heel, he walked away from her.

CHAPTER ELEVEN

FOR THE NEXT four days they remained locked in silent, seething battle. But they made almost comical efforts to be civil to one another in front of her mother, Patience and the staff. And Gael was an exceptional host on the occasions when they took her mother to a private gallery viewing in Barcelona and then to an open park showing of *Tosca*, both of which her mother lapped up with almost childlike joy.

But the moment they were alone his charming smile and drawling banter evaporated. He barely glanced at her as he busied himself with his newspaper or whatever meal he was consuming. The moment he deemed it acceptable he left the room, either to pound relentless laps in the swimming pool or to lock himself in his study.

Goldie had no such escape. On long walks over the estate her mother was growing to love, she endured probing questions and concerned looks. The only upside of the effort it took to maintain a happy face was that she fell into bed exhausted at the end of the day, with her sleep only disturbed at the crack of dawn by relentless morning sickness.

The day before Gael's brother's wedding—the last day of her mother's visit—she entered the dining room to find Gael pouring hot water into a fine bone china teacup. Adding two slices of lemon and a cube of sugar, he stirred it briefly before setting it down in front of her, along with a small plate of dry crackers.

'Drink this. Teresa swears by it for morning sickness,' he said gruffly.

Her surprised glance swung to his, but he was walking away to get himself an espresso. Expecting him to leave the room, since there was no one to entertain, she gulped at a hot mouthful when he sat down at the head of the table.

'Am I to assume that we're talking to each other now?' she asked, after a few minutes had passed and she'd drunk half the sweetened hot water. She was aware that her tone was a touch waspish, but she'd been unable to stem the hurt of the past few days.

'Talking has never been a problem for me. Arguing without purpose, on the other hand, bores me.'

Her breath shuddered out. 'So you either want to hear only what suits you or silence?'

He tossed back his espresso and set the cup down with a heavy hand. 'No, Goldie, the only subject I'm not prepared to argue about or compromise on is the subject of sex. And since that subject appears to be a ticking time bomb between us, I suggest you tread carefully.'

The cup trembled in her hand so she set it down. 'I know your mind isn't one-track like that—'

His harsh laugh fractured her words. 'Do you? I'm a red-blooded male, Goldie. One with a healthy sexual appetite and stringent views on fidelity. You're the woman who's taken my name and my ring but is refusing to share my bed. Since I don't intend to break my vows, I'm left with a huge, potentially insurmountable problem. So do you *really* think I'm overreacting?' he grated at her.

Her blush was fierce and all-encompassing. But then so was the ache that wouldn't budge from her heart. 'Do *you* expect *me* to have sex with you when you've accused me of marrying you just so I'll get my hands on your money?'

'Come off it, Goldie. Sex was off the table even before you signed on the dotted line. You just decided to keep it to yourself. You were biding your time before you dropped your little bombshell.'

'No, I wasn't—because I wasn't even thinking about it then. You left me in bed the first time we made love without a word. I woke up to a note that was tantamount to you telling me you'd made a mistake. And you think the natural progression from that, when we agreed to marry for the sake of our baby, automatically includes sex?'

A faint dull red tinged his cheekbones, but his expression remained rigid. 'I wasn't expecting you to be a virgin so, *sí*, I was a little…thrown. But I did return to you. Only you were asleep. I took the unselfish way of not waking you and chose to sleep in the spare bedroom. But my question still stands. You knew my views on fidelity before you married me, so what did you *think* was going to happen?'

'I expected we would talk about it. We never got

the chance to discuss it so neither of us knew where we stood.'

'What about now? Where *do* we stand?' he countered.

She shook her head. 'Right now we stand with me wondering why on earth you'd want to sleep with a shameless gold-digger who would barter her child for fifty million dollars!'

He shrugged, his eyes feverishly raking her face. 'The money means nothing to me, *guapa*,' he drawled softly. 'Having your body beneath mine again in bed would be worth more than twice that to me.'

'I do *not* want to sleep with you for money!'

'Too late—you have already signed the documents, remember?'

Her hands shook so hard she clenched them in her lap before he saw. 'Why are you so determined to think the worst of me, Gael?'

'I'm merely going by the evidence before me.'

'*What* evidence? My deplorable timing because I said yes right after you threw in your supposed sweetener?'

'You signed the document,' he sliced at her again.

'Yes, I signed it. So what? Was it some sort of test that I failed? Is there no room for the benefit of the doubt in your world?'

'That is up to you, Goldie.'

'How?'

His gaze moved past her face, down her throat, to the two-button opening of her white sleeveless sundress. 'Find a way.'

He left the dining room shortly after that.

On shaky feet she got up and went to the sideboard to replenish her cup with hot water. Her mother and Patience entered as she was heading back to her seat. Greetings were exchanged. And then she went back to avoiding her mother's probing stares.

After eating a piece of toast and half a banana without incident, she begged off when her mother invited her to the local market to shop for the souvenirs Gloria wanted to take back to the US. Feeling bad, she promised a mother-daughter lunch before her mother and Patience were taken to the airport for their evening flight.

Escaping to her room, Goldie paced, her mind darting over her conversation with Gael. How could something so seemingly straightforward have become such a jumbled mess?

Was she naive not to have considered that Gael would want a wife in *every* sense of the word after he'd gone out of his way to avoid her after the first time they'd made love? He claimed he'd returned after disappearing into the bathroom for longer than was normal. But his note the next morning had left very little doubt as to his feelings.

And he'd tried to fob her off with money then too!

She paused mid-stride. It was clear that money was the issue. Gael Aguilar was used to dealing with gold-diggers and scheming women. By signing the prenuptial agreement as it stood, she'd all but drawn a bullseye on her back.

Crossing to the bed, she grabbed her purse and searched for the document. There were pages and pages of it, all wrapped up in legalese. But she eventually found the clause she was looking for. Her heart leapt as she read and re-read it. Grabbing her phone, she did a quick search for local attorneys—those who practised in English as well as Spanish.

After making an appointment, she jumped off the bed and went in search of her mother. She breathed in relief when she caught her and Patience as they headed out.

'Is it too late to join you?'

Her mother turned around and smiled. 'Of course not!'

Asking Teresa to let Gael know she'd gone out with her mother, she joined them in the SUV.

The Friday market in Villa de Gracia was bustling, with exquisite trinkets and to-die-for souvenirs at every turn. It was easy for Goldie to leave her mother happily browsing and keep her appointment with the attorney. It took a good few minutes to explain to the ageing lawyer just what she wanted, and he seemed genuinely puzzled by her request. But eventually he called in his son, who agreed to draw up the requisite documents.

Twenty-five minutes later Goldie emerged from the attorney's office with a smile on her face.

'Find a way,' Gael had dared her.

She just had.

Gael was waiting on the front steps of the villa when they returned. The three women glanced at his face as the driver braked the SUV to a stop and the easy laughter in the vehicle died.

'Well, looks like someone's headed for the doghouse,'

Patience quipped under her breath. 'Goldie, honey, what did you *do* to the poor man?' the plump companion, originally from New Orleans, stage-whispered.

Goldie snorted. 'Sometimes I just need to breathe the wrong way.'

Muffled laughter ensued, quickly cut off as Gael strode to the car and opened the door.

'Everything okay, son?' her mother asked sweetly.

Gael jerked out a nod. '*Sí*, everything's fine, Gloria,' he responded, without taking his eyes off Goldie. 'Can I talk to you, *cara*?'

She could tell he was trying to keep his tone even, but the flames raging through his eyes and the white lines bracketing his mouth told a different story.

She pasted a smile on her face. 'Sure.'

He took her hand and led her into the house. Once inside, he crossed the large rotunda-shaped foyer and took the right set of sweeping wood and iron stairs that led to the second level.

'Gael—'

He stopped suddenly in the middle of the staircase and stared down at her. One hand reached out and brushed her lower lip. His fingers were shaking.

'You've been itching for an argument, *guapa*. And I'm about to give you the mother of them all. Just hang tight,' he snarled, low and deadly.

He resumed climbing, his steps quickening as they crested the stairs. It was all she could do to keep up with him as he moved to the west wing and entered his bedroom.

Goldie had only caught glimpses of Gael's suite,

which was connected to hers. She'd seen it when he'd come into her room on the night of their wedding.

Seeing it in all its glory for the first time, she stopped in the middle of the room. A rich, pale wood theme was everywhere, blended from ceiling to bed to floor, interspersed with a dark marble Goldie wanted to run her fingers over just to see if it was as warm and luxurious as it looked.

Of course all that passed through her mind in a split second before the man...her husband...shut the door with a decidedly repressed click and planted himself in front of her.

For several heartbeats he just stared at her. 'You went into town with your mother?'

Goldie blinked. 'Uh...yes?'

He breathed in, long and deep. 'You went into town with your mother, and then *went to see a divorce attorney*?' he seethed with white-hot fury.

Oh, hell. Her heart lurched. 'What? No—!'

'You were seen, Goldie! The attorney's office confirmed it. So did my driver.'

He started to whirl away, one hand spiking viciously through his hair. He stopped both actions halfway through and launched himself back in front of her. He looked paler than before, a vein jumping frantically at his temple as he glared at her.

'Is this your answer when things don't go your way? Is this your way of trying to get my attention, to bend me to your will?'

She shook her head. 'You've got it wrong. Just let me ex—'

He pointed a finger at her. 'I *won't* grant you a divorce. We agreed to five years. You're going to give me those five years, and not a day less. You *do* understand that, don't you, Goldie? You *do* get that anything less and I'll make sure you're locked in a court battle you'll have no hope of emerging from for another five years after that.'

She exhaled, exasperation eating her alive. 'Well, no, I *don't* get that. *If* I want a divorce you'll have to give me one when the five years are up. That's the agreement. But—'

'But nothing! *Santa Maria*, we've been married less than a week and one argument sends you running to a— Wait... *If?*'

She tried to resist rolling her eyes. She failed. 'I'm going to explain myself to you now, Gael. Are you ready to listen?'

His brow was thunderous. 'I'm not a child, Goldie. Tell me what I need to know.'

She bit her tongue against a curt answer. 'I've told you I don't want your money.'

His nostrils flared but he remained silent.

'So I went to see an attorney to give it away.'

His eyes widened. 'What?'

'The agreement says that on each wedding anniversary I get the sum you promised wired to my account. I got the attorney to divide that money five ways—two-fifths will go to charities here in Barcelona and two-fifths to charities in the States. The fifth portion will go to a local performing arts community near where I live in Trenton.' She reached into her purse, withdrew the document and held it out to him. 'Here—see for yourself.'

Mild shock blanketing his face, he took the document from her, read it with lightning speed.

Then he frowned at her. 'You're giving away all the money?'

'All of it.'

'And did you happen to discuss divorce with this attorney while you were getting this done?' he demanded, his eyes still a touch wild.

'No, Gael. I didn't. The D-word didn't once pass my lips. You said to find a way. I found a way.'

He exhaled, his breath decidedly shaky as he bunched up the document and flung it over his shoulder. 'Why the hell didn't you say that?'

'You were on a roll. I tried to stop you, but you seemed intent on flattening me.'

He paced in a tight circle without once taking his eyes off her. '*Dios mio.* Why do I you let you drive me so crazy?' he seethed quietly.

She shrugged. 'You drive *yourself* crazy. You don't need my help.'

He gave a deep, vicious growl before he lunged for her. Fingers spiked into her hair, angled her head, a nanosecond before his mouth smashed down on hers. He kissed her hungrily, deeply, then ripped his mouth from hers a minute later.

'You found a way?' he whispered roughly.

'I found a way.'

He leaned his forehead against hers, his eyes boring into her own. 'Does that mean you want to be with me, Goldie?' he demanded, his voice hoarse with need. 'Truly be mine?'

'Yes,' she replied simply.

Because her need for him *was* that simple. She'd been a fool to imagine that she could erase it out of the equation—that she would be content to sleep next door to him for five long years. Even if it were true that Gael would tire of her after six short weeks, she was still going to take that time with him.

The kiss he delivered after her answer in the affirmative was bliss-inducing. Her purse fell off her shoulder and was forgotten. The hem of her sundress was gripped in a tight hold, pulled over her head and dropped to the floor, leaving her in the white bikini set she'd planned to wear for lounging by the poolside that morning.

Gael caressed his way down her jaw, her throat and shoulders. Cupping those, he turned her around and groaned, low and deep.

'*Amante*, you're so beautiful.'

The throaty words drew a delicious shiver from her, making her tremble in his arms. His fingers catching the long ties of her bikini top, he pulled them free and turned her around. Eyes turned burnished gold devoured her seconds before his hands resumed their caress. A deeper tremble seized her as he cupped her breasts and squeezed. Her hand rose to grip his waist.

She needed to hold on to him. It was a desire and a necessity. Her gaze rose to meet his and her breath caught at the ferocious hunger in his eyes. Unable to resist, she stood on tiptoe and pressed her mouth to his. His hands left her breasts to gather her close. He groaned when her chest pressed into his. Clever fingers made short work of the bottom half of the bikini. Then, naked, she was once again caught in his arms.

After an age of glorious kissing, Gael picked her up and carried her to his king-sized bed. Quick and efficient movements relieved him of his clothes and then he prowled onto the bed, sleek and magnificent next to her.

From cheek to neck, cleavage to midriff, every inch of her skin was covered in open-mouthed kisses, while over and over his fingers drifted over her abdomen where their baby nestled.

Suddenly he snapped his head up, eyes narrowed. 'Did you take your prenatal vitamins this morning?' he asked.

Goldie curbed the need to smile. 'Yes.'

A brisk nod. 'Did you have a good breakfast?'

'Yes.'

He completed another circling caress over her belly. 'Are you hungry now? The pregnancy book says you should eat little and often. Can I get you anything?'

She suppressed a groan of frustration, sliding her hands over his shoulders, glorying in the muscles that bunched at her touch. 'I'm fine, Gael. I don't need anything. No—actually, scratch that. I need *you*. Only you.'

His grin was full and unfettered, snagging a tight string around her heart. Bending his head, he placed a deep, reverent kiss on her belly before he began to kiss his way lower.

Goldie tried and failed to stop the hot blushes that rolled over her at the expert attention he delivered between her legs. Much too soon she was crying out and soaring high. Still buzzing, she moaned as he rose over her, kissed her lips and caught her hands together above her head.

'Open your legs for me, *querida*,' he commanded throatily.

She obeyed wholeheartedly.

'Now, look at me. Show me your beautiful eyes.'

Her breath still unsteady from the aftershocks of her climax, she lifted her gaze. He caught it easily, his eyes pinning her as effectively as his body pinned hers.

One hand holding hers captive, he used the other to guide himself into her. They both groaned as pleasure surged, pure and dizzying. Without the restriction of a condom the pleasure was more intense—a fact Gael gutturally attested to a minute after the sensational thought flew across her brain.

'I want it like this from now on. Always. I can never go back.'

'Yes…' she readily agreed, already on a set course to flame-hot bliss.

He increased his tempo, need dictating the pace as he thrust deeper inside her. On another thick groan he lowered his head and fused her mouth with his. Tongues melding, breath mingling, they celebrated their coming together with unfettered passion, then collapsed into each other's arms as ecstasy flung them into nirvana.

Once their breaths quietened he speared his fingers through her hair and angled her face to his.

'This time when I go to the bathroom be assured that I will return,' he mock growled.

Goldie laughed, her heart lifting with a sensation she didn't want to name just yet. 'Okay.'

He left her for a minute, returned with a warmed towel. After seeing to her, he returned it to the bath-room. Her breath caught all over again as she watched his gladiator-like body move towards her. She might not be in this position for the whole of the five years they'd committed to one another but, boy, she intended to enjoy every minute of the time she did have.

'Dare I ask what's going on in that brain of yours?' he drawled.

She grimaced. 'I'm thinking we need to get up soon, before Mom comes knocking. It's almost time for them to head to the airport.'

'Right. Nothing like the thought of my mother-in-law catching me defiling her daughter to kill my buzz.'

She laughed. He joined in.

She felt another life-defining twinge of her heart.

By the time they got up to get dressed, ten minutes later, Goldie was beginning to fear the changes her emo-tions were going through...

CHAPTER TWELVE

GAEL ADJUSTED THE SLEEVES of his morning suit and resisted the urge to glance at his watch for the third time
in as many minutes.

'Goldie, we're going to be late.'

They were expected at Alejandro's villa at noon—an
hour before the ceremony started.

'I... I'm almost there.'

He frowned. He didn't understand her need to keep
a separate bedroom now she was sharing his bed.
Granted, it had only been one night, but her half-hearted
agreement when he'd suggested this morning that she
move her things into his suite had irritated him.

Now, with the added tension of the impending ceremony and the inevitable face-to-face with his father,
his nape felt tight. Hell, his whole body was on a knife-
edge.

He whirled from the window.

And was confronted with a vision.

Dios mio, she was breathtaking! With the time she'd
spent in the sun, her *café-au-lait* skin was almost as dark
as his own, making her violet eyes stunning luminous
pools. But the flush of pregnancy had added a glow that

made it impossible for him to take his eyes off her. With her carefully styled but already a little wild corkscrew curls, and her body draped in a shoulder-baring, floor-length dress, she looked as divine as an angel. She wore the pearl earrings she'd worn on their wedding day, but her throat was bare. She was radiant enough—didn't need further adornment.

Gael wasn't sure why the memory had chosen that moment to return, but his insides snagged hard as he recalled how he'd felt when he'd received the call from his driver about her visit to the attorney's office. The hour he'd paced until her return had felt like the blackest of his life.

Which puzzled and disturbed the hell out of him.

Telling himself it was just because she carried his child rang a little hollow. Now that he'd accepted he was to be a father, it was a position he was looking forward to. If nothing else, he wanted to conquer the demons that howled at him that the seed he came from was poisoned. He didn't believe that any more. He would be better. Their child would be cared for and cherished.

What he'd felt yesterday had been something different altogether. He'd been afraid of losing *Goldie*, not the child she carried. And if that wasn't unnerving enough, the sharp swing of his mood in the opposite direction when she'd revealed the reason for her visit had been so acute he'd been almost dizzy with it.

That latter feeling had continued to cascade through him all through the night and to this moment. For the first time in his life Gael didn't know whether he wanted to face the problem head-on, as usual, or back away from it.

'Um…say something? *Anything?*'

He chose to back away. 'It's way past time to go.'

She grimaced. 'Right. Fine.'

He smiled. 'And you look magnificent, *querida.*'

When she reached him she punched him lightly in the arm. He responded by catching her offending hand and trailing his lips across the back of it. And as he was rewarded with a smile as luminescent as her eyes Gael felt himself swing towards that unknown high. Felt himself lose the solid ground beneath his feet.

Shaking his head, he took a deep breath and escorted her outside.

They just needed to get today over and done with. Then he could make the time to examine these *feelings* that had taken hold of him.

The limo ride to Alejandro's adjoining estate took fifteen minutes, and he welcomed the time to answer Goldie's subtle questions about his relationship with his brother. As he answered her he realised it was another first. He didn't find talking about Alejandro as difficult as he once had, and the half-brother he'd once believed he would never willingly accept had become more of a family symbol in his mind than his own mother.

His jaw tightened as he thought of his mother and her threatened visit. Gael hadn't gone out of his way to keep Goldie's pregnancy a secret—he'd told Alejandro and Elise—but he knew his mother kept tabs on him through his household staff. So he hadn't been surprised

when she'd called yesterday and dropped subtle hints
until he'd divulged the news.

Her immediate announcement that she intended to
visit had rubbed him the wrong way. But, no matter
how disappointed and bitter he felt over her behaviour,
he'd never rejected any overtures from her.

'Gael, if you clench your jaw any harder it'll snap,'
Goldie said gently from beside him. 'Same goes for
my hand.'

He exhaled sharply, released the tight grip he'd un-
consciously placed on her hand and kissed it better. *'Lo
siento.* I should warn you—my father will most likely
be at the wedding.'

She nodded, her sexy curls bounced. 'And...?'

'And I haven't seen him for over ten years.' He
shrugged. 'I can't say how things will go.'

'Okay.' She frowned. 'Your mother won't be there,
will she?'

He gave a bitter laugh and shook his head. 'No, but
she's coming to the villa tomorrow.'

Her eyes widened. 'Does she know about the baby?'

'Yes, but not about us being married.'

'Do the rest of your family know?'

'I told Andro and Elise last week. As much as I relish being a pain in Alejandro's backside, I didn't want
our news to take over their day.'

Her smile warmed him, made him feel less edgy. It
felt like the most natural thing in the world to slide his
hand around her shoulders and pull her close. Her face
turned up to his immediately, and he lost himself in the
sensation of kissing her.

His driver's throat-clearing announced their arrival and Gael pulled back reluctantly.

'You owe me another dozen of those when we get home.'

She rolled her eyes, but her smile widened as she slid her hand into his and let him help her out.

Alejandro's villa was almost a carbon copy of his, bar a few minor details—like the absence of a climbing vine in the courtyard and the presence of an art studio built for Elise. His soon-to-be sister-in-law had become an overnight Manga-writing sensation when she'd sold her thirty-story collection for a fortune last year. Now retired from her previous work as a PR consultant, she was pursuing a flourishing full-time Manga-creating career.

Alejandro was descending the stairs when they entered. Gael locked eyes with his half-brother and noted that the acrimony he'd spent years nursing was almost non-existent. In their own stilted way they'd managed to forge a bond—one Gael suddenly hoped would grow stronger.

He eyed his older brother's state of semi-undress with a mocking smirk. 'Are you sure you're getting married in an hour? You look like you've just escaped a drunken sailor's bachelor party.'

Alejandro's mouth quirked in a half-smile. 'This is the result when I'm not allowed to see my fiancée for almost twenty-four hours. Whoever came up with that idiotic tradition deserves to hang.'

His dark hazel eyes shifted to Goldie. Lingered.

Although Gael knew the depth of feeling between

his half-brother and his almost-wife, something very much like jealousy shifted inside him. 'Goldie, this is Alejandro, my bear of a brother. Andro—meet Goldie.'

'Pleased to meet you. And congratulations on both accounts,' Andro drawled.

Goldie smiled and held out her hand. Alejandro's eyes widened infinitesimally before he took her hand and brushed his lips over the back of it.

Gael bristled.

Andro sent him a *payback's a bitch* wink.

He laughed, knowing he deserved the payback for flirting with Elise the first time they'd met.

'Okay. Well played,' he replied.

Goldie looked from him to Andro. 'Am I missing something?'

Gael shook his head. 'Nothing worth mentioning.'

Alejandro laughed under his breath, then his expression sobered. When he glanced at a nearby clock Gael was sure he growled under his breath.

'Do you need my help with anything, or shall we leave you to your growling and staff-frightening?' he mocked.

'If I wasn't absolutely certain Elise would have my hide, I'd sink a double shot of bourbon right about now.' He cast another look at the clock.

Gael laughed. 'Good luck with that. I'll see you at the altar.'

Alejandro nodded, started to walk away and then stopped. '*Mi hermano*, I should warn you—our father is here. He arrived early. You can avoid him if you want, but if you're headed for the salon he'll be in there.'

His eyes narrowed and Gael saw the same ruthlessness that coursed through his veins reflected in his brother's eyes.

'For Elise's sake I would prefer it if you kept your reunion brawl-free—*entiendes*?'

Everything inside Gael tightened, but he managed a nod before his brother walked away. Gael remained where he stood, his senses once more on the finest of edges.

'We don't have to go in there if you don't want to.'

He started, having momentarily forgotten his wife's presence. Resolutely, he shook his head. 'This meeting has been inevitable and it's long overdue. Besides, I have a couple of things to get off my chest,' he said.

He saw the trepidation in her face, wished he could soothe it. But the strides carrying him into the salon demanded all his attention.

Gael's eyes zeroed in on him immediately—saw the moment his father sensed his presence. He stood next to his wife, Alejandro's mother, who was seated with a coffee in her hand.

Tomas Aguilar's gaze sharpened, then widened with a mixture of shock and shame before his expression was neutralised. Gael wished that evidence of shame soothed the part of him he'd for a long time denied was still hurting. Perhaps a few months ago—before Tomas had struck up his illicit affair with his mother once more—it *would* have gone some way to soothe the rejection.

But not now.

He strolled forward until he reached the two of them.

Evita Aguilar glanced up at him, her face reflecting neither acceptance nor rejection. For a moment he felt sorry for her, having tied her destiny to a man with such low scruples. But she averted her gaze and her opinion ceased to matter.

His eyes reconnected with Tomas Aguilar's and again he saw that momentary flash of shame, this time accompanied by regret.

'It's good to see you...son,' his father said in his native tongue.

Shock held Gael rigid, then he replied tersely, 'English, please. My wife doesn't speak Spanish.'

Both Tomas and Evita started.

'Your *wife*?' His father recovered first, his gaze swinging to Goldie.

'*Sí,*' Gael responded.

After observing her for a few charged seconds, he inclined his head. 'I'm Tomas, and this is my wife, Evita.'

Goldie's smile was a little guarded, but sincere. 'Hello, I'm Goldie.'

Gael's smile felt tight. 'Now that we have the pleasantries over and done with, enjoy the rest of your day.'

His father opened his mouth as if he wanted to say something. Then he glanced down at his wife and shut it again.

More bitterness dredged through Gael. Tightening his hold on Goldie, he led her away.

'I thought you were going to talk to him?'

'So did I, but I find that even that isn't worth doing any more.'

They walked through the salon's French doors and

out onto a wide terrace. Beyond the large white columns rolled a sea of green grass, and in the centre was displayed the wedding arch where the ceremony was to be held. Fifty white-linen-draped chairs were divided on either side of the arch for the guests, the first of whom were appearing in limos and luxury cars at the bottom of the long driveway.

'Are you sure?'

Gael was certain the answer was yes until he opened his mouth. 'Maybe not.'

'He looked like he wanted to say something. So maybe let *him* do the talking?'

He glanced down at her with a slight frown. 'Only a short while ago he loomed large over my life, dictated my choices without me realising it.' He shrugged. 'But not so much any more.'

Gael suspected the feeling had something to do with the woman in front of him. Yet another thing to be examined later.

'All the same, you have a chance to get rid of the toxin once and for all. Do you want to look back and wonder if it would've been better to reconnect, to find some answers for yourself?'

Gael remembered hinting at something similar to Alejandro last year. At the time he'd blithely dropped a suggestion that his brother reconnect with the parents he'd walked away from. He knew Alejandro's visit to Seville hadn't been easy. Just as the contemplation of today hadn't been easy for Gael.

Slowly, he nodded. 'Maybe. Now, enough about this.

You owe me a dozen kisses. Make good on one of them now, please.'

He was seconds from losing his mind from a kiss alone when footsteps pulled them apart.

Alejandro, followed by his parents, had stepped out onto the terrace, followed by the first of the guests. Waiters were serving mimosas and champagne to keep the guests refreshed until the organ struck up.

When it did, Gael led Goldie to the front row and stepped beside his brother.

The ceremony went without a hitch. Elise smiled widely when Gael welcomed her into the family. Then he watched as his new sister-in-law and his wife fell into instant friendship.

All through the ceremony he'd caught his father's eyes on him. And after countless trips to the dance floor with Goldie—because he didn't want to miss any opportunity to hold her in his arms—she pushed him towards Tomas.

'It's time, Gael. Come and find me when you're done.'

He caught her before she could walk away. 'No, you come and find *me* in ten minutes. I'm guessing that's about how long I'll be able to stand it before things head south.'

She nodded. 'Okay—deal.'

He watched her sway off the dance floor and immediately be accosted by Elise.

His father was looking his way when he turned.

Gael snagged a whisky from a passing waiter before stepping out of the giant marquee onto the green grass.

Above him the night sky twinkled with a thousand stars. But he was too on edge to appreciate the view.

Tomas joined him a minute later.

Gael turned his head and met eyes the same colour as his own. 'I hated you for a very long time.'

He didn't see any reason to mince his words. A second later he realised that he'd spoken in the past tense and spoken in English, because he wasn't ready to have another thing in common with the man whose blood ran through his veins.

A wave of pain and regret passed over Tomas's face. 'I know. And I deserved all of it. For what I did to you, and to your brother, you have every right to hate me.'

'But you're still doing it, aren't you? With my mother?' he accused, and a deep cloying emotion he recognised as pain roughened his voice.

Tomas shook his head. 'No, I'm not.'

Gael snorted. 'I spoke to my mother two weeks ago. She was going to see you.'

'Yes, I met with her to end it.'

Gael stared hard at his father, wondering whether to believe him or not.

'I should never have started things with your mother again. It was selfish. But after Andro came to see me last year I thought you and I might reconnect too… I couldn't summon the courage to reach out directly to you. So I called Katerina.'

Gael cursed under his breath.

Tomas shrugged. 'I think you know that I'm far from perfect. I would go so far as to call myself unworthy of being a father to both my sons. But you and Alejandro have grown into exceptional men, and I remain selfish enough to want to be a part of your lives. I would be honoured to be in your life at some point beyond today, but if you don't think that's a possibility let me tell you now that I'm proud of you.'

Something tugged in his chest. Gael fought to resist it.

'You're *proud*? You told me I was a *mistake*—that I should never have been born! Because of you I don't trust anyone… I don't know how to *love* anyone. I'm a bastard who shouldn't exist.'

Tomas paled, his eyes anguished as he stared at Gael. 'But your relationship with your brother is thriving, and you have a beautiful wife who clearly worsh —'

His laughter cut off his father's words. 'A wife I'm incapable of loving because I don't know how. A wife I've paid for. Because on the night I found out you were still sniffing around my mother I was so angry that I slaked my anger and lust on an innocent woman. After that she fell pregnant with my child, and now I'm tied to her for life—'

The ragged gasp behind him tore through to his very soul.

Even before he turned around Gael knew the landscape of his life had changed irrevocably.

Because six feet behind him Goldie stood, ghost-pale and pain-ravaged, her eyes lost pools as she shook her head slowly.

'*Dios mio*… Goldie.' He started towards her.

Her hands flew out. 'No. Stay away from me!'

He couldn't fathom ever doing that. So he took another step. She stumbled back, her heel catching on the grass.

It was Tomas who went to her aid. Tomas who helped her to her feet with a gentle touch that turned Gael's stomach.

Get your hands off her! he wanted to scream. But the words wouldn't come. His life was too busy flashing before his eyes.

But he had to act. He couldn't lose her.

Unable to believe what was happening, he tried again. 'Please, *querida. Por favor*, let me ex—'

'I swear, if you take one more step towards me I'll scream the place down. And I'll leave you to explain to your brother what went down here.'

They stood frozen, the three of them, in a twisted tableau.

After a handful of seconds Tomas turned to him. 'Let her go, Gael,' his father said to him in Spanish. 'Emotions are too high right now. You can try and repair things later.'

Every instinct screamed against his taking his father's advice. But Goldie's raised chin and her aggressive stance spelled a no-go zone he would find impossible to breach. Still, his chest felt on fire with the idea of letting her go.

'*Amante*, please...' he tried again.

'I'm leaving, Gael, and I don't want you to come with me.'

He glanced at his father. Saw a tiny nod from Tomas.

His ragged sigh felt like a gasp of death. 'I'll tell the

driver to take you home. I'll be there in an hour, maybe two. Will…will that be enough time?'

Dios, please let her say yes. He couldn't stand to be away longer than that.

Her mouth twisted. 'More than enough.'

With those two words his wife turned on her spiky heels and walked away.

And with each step she took Gael's senses screamed at him that he was making the biggest mistake of his life.

CHAPTER THIRTEEN

GOLDIE HAD NO RECOLLECTION of what she'd packed or how long it had taken for the driver to deliver her to the airport. But somehow she'd managed to talk to a ticket agent and buy a ticket home.

She still had a couple of days before the last leg of filming commenced for *Soul's Triumph*, for which she thanked God. Because the way she felt right now—the way her heart screamed as if it was being ripped out with each breath she took—she didn't think she could utter one line, never mind a few hundred.

She needed the comfort of home, of her mother, even though she would need to turn around and come right back to Spain in two days to join the cast and crew. Even though Gael would most likely still be here.

She just couldn't bear to be here right now. Because somewhere between his threats and his mockery and his smiles and his exceptional lovemaking she'd fallen in love with the man whose child she carried.

Goldie was too weary to pinpoint when exactly it had happened. It had happened. And even before she'd dared to hope that her fragile feelings might be returned he'd dashed hope in the most devastating way possible.

She only had herself to blame. Everything that had happened from the moment Gael had stepped into that alley six weeks ago had been her fault.

He'd made her no promises, save for telling her that he desired her and wanted the child she carried, and she'd foolishly chosen to let her heart loose in the frantic hope for love.

Squeezing her eyes shut and turning her head away from the curious passenger next to her, she pressed her fist to her mouth as tears fell.

Maybe the newness of her love meant she could salvage her heart?

Dream on, her shattered heart mocked.

She'd fallen hook, line and sinker.

There was no going back.

Gael tried to outstare his mother-in-law as she bodily barred her front door.

'Sorry, son. She doesn't want to see you.'

There was nothing remotely remorseful in her tone. In fact her body bristled with enough quiet fury for him to realise where Goldie got her strength from.

'Gloria, I just want to talk to her for five minutes.' He used his most reasonable negotiating tone, despite wanting to roar and plead and beg.

Gloria Beckett folded her arms. 'She flew six thousand miles to get away from you. Hoping that a five-minute conversation will fix things is a touch foolish, don't you think?' she challenged.

Suitably chastised, he nodded. 'I'm willing to do whatever it takes, however long it takes. Can you please tell her that?'

He received a shrug in return, and the light violet eyes narrowed on him as he fought the urge to pace. A few times he opened his mouth to speak. Every time, Gloria's chin went up higher, daring him to utter more damning words.

Gael bit his tongue against cursing and tried to see past the woman's shoulder into the house that harboured the woman he loved—the woman he couldn't bear to be apart from for one more second. Gloria's subtle shifting told him he was pushing it.

He shoved his fingers through his hair and tried one more time. 'Is everything okay with her?'

Gloria tossed her blonde head. 'Are you asking about my daughter or about the baby?'

'I'm asking about my *wife*. About *our child*.'

'You should have thought about them before you messed up.'

Spikes of anguish ripped wounds through his heart. 'You're right. I messed up. Badly. But I want… I *need* the chance to fix it. *Por favor?*' he added gruffly when she remained intransigent.

Her stare bored into him for depressingly long seconds before she sighed. 'I'll tell her what you said, son. But don't hold your breath. My daughter is made of strong stuff. She may be bent a little out of shape right now, but she's not broken. If she learns to stand again without you, then you'll have missed your chance.'

His heart dropped to his feet as she stepped back and slammed the door in his face.

He raised his hand to knock again, then froze when he heard the ragged sobs coming from within.

He'd spent the last twenty-four hours in hell. But the woman crying inside the house—the woman his heart yearned for more than it wanted to beat—was hurting. And it was his fault. His being here was hurting her even more.

And yet Gael couldn't leave. Staggering away from the door, he stumbled down the front step and sank onto it. Time ticked by, marched on. He couldn't move.

A light rain began to fall. He watched the droplets form on his arms and drip down his fingers. His numbness kept him insulated. Gael looked up when his driver stepped from the limo and started walking towards him with a blanket. He shook his head once, fiercely, sending the man backtracking. He didn't deserve to feel warm. Besides, compared to the chill in his heart the rain was nothing.

Midnight slowly ticked by. He knew because a clock chimed inside the house.

When he heard a noise behind him he wondered if someone's house pet had chosen to join him in misery.

'Are you trying to make some sort of point by freezing to death on my doorstep?'

Gael stood and jerked round. One lunge up the steps and he was standing in front of her.

'Goldie…*mi amor*…please give me a chance to explain.' He wanted to touch her but he didn't dare—didn't want to risk her bolting back inside.

'I think what I heard was clear enough. You bought me and you don't think you can love me.'

He shook his head, spreading a few raindrops.

She wiped a drop from her cheek, her movements jerky.

'No... I mean, yes, that's what I said. But I didn't mean it. Not like that.'

He stopped and inhaled. How could words fail him, today of all days, when his life depended on it?

'What I meant was, I knew you were leaning towards a yes to my proposal even before I offered you the money and the movie roles. I tagged them on because I wanted to be able to tell myself you'd chosen to marry me because of money.'

Her brows clamped in a frown. 'Why?' she asked, bewildered.

'Hearing that you weren't wanted, that you're a mistake, even once, isn't something you can brush under the carpet and forget easily. Alejandro and I are true brothers now, but there was a time when I thought he was the same as our father in his contempt of me. Having two out of your three closest blood relations reject you as a child is...painful. I convinced myself I was okay with it, but it wasn't until lately—until *you*—that I realised I'd let it cloud a lot of my life's decisions.'

He stopped and took a deep breath.

'I have a confession to make.'

Her eyes grew more wary. 'Yes?'

'I was at Othello on another audition hunt when I heard you performing. I was stunned by you. But then I heard that casting director proposition you.'

She gasped. 'That's why you were so nasty to me when we met? Why you would look at me sometimes with that judgemental look in your eyes?'

He sighed and nodded. 'I saw him touch you, thought you were agreeable to what he'd proposed, but I know now I must have misheard.'

'I didn't understand what he was asking me at first. When I did, I told him to go to hell.'

'I guessed as much. But much later. I'm sorry, Goldie.'

Her lips pursed. 'You were saying about your past clouding your judgement...?'

He nodded. 'When you wouldn't share my bed I thought it was because I wasn't good enough for you, so I lashed out at you. I'm sorry, *mi amor*. I didn't buy you. I threw money at you so I could make myself feel better, tell myself that yearning for you the way I did was okay because I had controlled your entry into my life. It was wrong, Goldie, and I'd give anything to turn back time and unsay what I said about you to my father.'

He watched, cursed as tears slowly filled her eyes.

'*Dios mio*, please don't cry.'

'I won't lie to you, Gael. You hurt me.'

Pain sliced his insides. 'I'll fix it, Goldie. I swear with everything I am I'll spend the rest of my life un-doing this hurt.'

Her mouth trembled. 'How?' she croaked.

'Let me love you. Let me earn the right to worship you. You and our child. I'll do whatever you want.'

She licked her lips. 'What if what I want...what I *need*...is you?'

A tremble seized him that had nothing to do with

the chilled wet shirt clinging to his back. 'Then take me. I'm yours.'

'Not until I know…until I'm sure how you feel.'

'How I…? *I love you.* I adore you.'

Her breath caught. 'Please say that again, Gael.'

He closed his eyes, dared to take her hands, bring them to his lips in a reverent kiss. 'I love you, Goldie Aguilar. It may be a new love, but I promise you it's strong, it's yours, and it *will* stand the test of time.'

She freed her hands to cup his face. 'Oh, Gael. I love you too.'

His eyes sprang open. 'You *love* me?'

'Yes. And my love is just as new as yours. I love you, and I'm willing to take a chance on us nurturing each other's love, if you want.'

'*Si!* I most definitely want.'

She smiled. His heart threatened to burst out of his chest.

She threw her arms around him and stood on tiptoe. 'Kiss me, Gael.'

It was his turn to smile. '*Dios*, you don't need to ask twice. If I remember correctly, you owe me ten kisses.'

'And I would've delivered if you hadn't thrown a spanner in the works.'

His face sobered. '*Lo siento, mi amor.* Forgive me.'

'All is forgiven.'

She fell into his arms again. When they finally parted their eyes were misted with tears.

'Take me home, Gael. Please.'

He nodded solemnly. 'It would be my honour, *mi mujer.*' He swung her up in his arms and started off the porch. About to step off, he paused. 'What about your mother?'

'She knows where my heart is…that I belong where you are.'

His head dropped until their foreheads touched. 'Goldie, I promise I will never make you regret that.'

She settled one hand over his heart, the other over her stomach, where their baby grew.

'And we promise to love and cherish you. For ever.'

EPILOGUE

BY UNANIMOUS AGREEMENT, voted on by their entire family, they held the wedding of their hearts two weeks after their daughter was born. Melina Aguilar lay nestled lovingly in her parents' arms as they renewed their vows in front of a much bigger, much happier congregation at the cathedral in Barcelona. Beneath centuries of history and stained-glass windows, they repeated the vows they'd uttered in that small chapel on Gael's estate.

Alejandro acted as his best man, and took delight in ribbing his brother mercilessly. And they stepped out into the late December evening to the sound of church bells and Christmas carols being sung in Spanish and English.

At the kerb, a vintage car stood waiting, beyond which a police cordon had been set up to keep back the screaming fans who shouted Goldie's name.

Soul's Triumph had been released to huge box office success three months before, and Goldie had become an overnight sensation. She'd been inundated with roles, but had elected to make only one movie a year, to free her to spend the rest of her time being a wife and mother—the two roles she cherished above all else.

She stopped long enough to wave to her fans before she got into the car, which was festooned not just with wedding decorations but also with holly and dozens of sprigs of mistletoe, some of which were also strung along the inside roof. Not that the couple needed any excuse to kiss on the long ride back to the villa once their daughter had fallen into a dreamy nap.

Goldie wrinkled her nose when Gael released her after another long, heady kiss, and indicated the mistletoe. 'Sorry about this. I tried to discourage my mother from doing it.'

Gael laughed. 'So did I with *my* mother—but I think we knew the moment those two got together that we didn't stand a chance.' He flicked a finger at the mistletoe. 'Although I'm not sure whether to be concerned that they believe I need a reason to kiss my wife, or to thank them for supplying me with so many opportunities to do so.'

He pulled her close once more and thoroughly explored her mouth.

They'd chosen to keep their reception small, for family and close friends only. And they arrived back at the house and alighted to join Alejandro and a very pregnant Elise. She was just over seven months, due on Valentine's Day—a fact which was a source of endless mocking ammunition for Gael against his brother.

The brothers had grown closer in the months following their respective marriages, and Goldie counted Elise not just as a sister-in-law but as a friend.

Goldie smiled at her now, as Elise joined her in the hallway and held out her arms for Melina.

Elise waited until the men were headed for the salon before she leaned in close. 'I think Gael has another role up his sleeve for you.' She winked.

Goldie laughed. 'Oh, really?'

Elise nodded. 'I heard him talking. He was asking Alejandro when it would be best to start trying for baby number two.'

Goldie rolled her eyes. 'And do I need two guesses as to what Andro's response was?'

Elise grinned. 'He said, "Immediately, of course."'

Both women laughed, causing their husbands to turn back and stare.

'What's going on?' Gael asked, making his way back to slide both arms around her.

Goldie smiled and kissed him. 'Nothing you need to worry about. Just yet.'

Both Alejandro and Gael groaned. Elise grinned unrepentantly and joined her husband. Goldie watched him tenderly touch Melina's cheek before he caressed his wife's rounded belly.

Gael's arms tightened around her, snagging her attention. She looked up into her husband's eyes. 'I love you. Thank you for marrying me again.'

'I'd marry you every day if I could.'

They kissed until their respective mothers walked past, clearing their throats loudly.

Gael and his mother had found their way back to each other after the end of her short affair with Tomas

Aguilar. There was still a little tension all round, but hearts and souls were slowly healing.

Grinning now, Gael and Goldie joined the rest of their family and their closest friends in the large salon for traditional Spanish Christmas tapas and drinks.

As toasts were given and presents exchanged, Goldie saw a look pass between Gael and Alejandro—powerful and visceral and filled with the affection they'd been denied as children but had found in abundance as husbands and brothers.

* * * * *

Don't miss the first part of Maya Blake's
RIVAL BROTHERS *duet*
A DEAL WITH ALEJANDRO
Available now!

If you enjoyed this story, check out these
other great reads from Maya Blake
THE DI SIONE SECRET BABY
SIGNED OVER TO SANTINO
A DIAMOND DEAL WITH THE GREEK
BRUNETTI'S SECRET SON
Available now!

#3481 A DI SIONE FOR THE GREEK'S PLEASURE
The Billionaire's Legacy
by Kate Hewitt

Natalia hasn't left the Di Sione estate in years, but must retrieve her grandfather's lost book of poems from formidable tycoon Angelos Mena—who's just mistaken her for his daughter's nanny! Angelos offers untold pleasure—but will he take her heart?

#3482 THE GREEK'S CHRISTMAS BRIDE
Christmas with a Tycoon
by Lynne Graham

The conditions of cynical bachelor Apollo Metraxis's inheritance force him to marry! Pixie Robinson's debts leave her defenseless—but her untouched vulnerability on their wedding night strikes a chord in Apollo's heart. And then he discovers that she's carrying *two* Metraxis heirs!

#3483 A ROYAL VOW OF CONVENIENCE
by Sharon Kendrick

Fleeing royal scrutiny places Sophie under the searing gaze of notorious billionaire Rafe Carter, who can't resist a forbidden taste of his chef. But when her identity is revealed, Rafe is duty bound to rescue the beautiful princess...with a convenient vow!

#3484 MARRIED FOR THE SHEIKH'S DUTY
Brides for Billionaires
by Tara Pammi

Sheikh Zayn Al-Ghamdi's reputation has already been damaged by scandal—so when Amalia Christensen blackmails him, he has to make her his *temporary* fiancée! But Amalia unleashes a hunger in Zayn that tempts him to take their relationship from business to bedroom...

#3485 THE PRINCE'S PREGNANT MISTRESS

Heirs Before Vows

by Maisey Yates

"I'm pregnant." It takes two words to see Prince Raphael DeSantis bound to a *waitress*. Now to prevent an international incident, Raphael must marry his mistress! But heartsore Bailey won't come willingly. Raphael must seduce Bailey Harper into submission...

#3486 THE GUARDIAN'S VIRGIN WARD

One Night With Consequences

by Caitlin Crews

Domineering Spaniard Izar Agustin couldn't have imagined that his ward, innocent Liliana Girard Brooks, would become such an alluring woman. One night of sensual abandon shows Liliana the unconscious desires of her body... But the consequences of that night bind them together...forever!

#3487 THE DESERT KING'S SECRET HEIR

Secret Heirs of Billionaires

by Annie West

Surrounded by society's glitterati, Arden Wills is confronted with her first and only love, Idris Baddour—a man she never knew was a sheikh! When their ardent kiss is blasted across the world's media, Arden's secret comes to light—the Sheikh has a son!

#3488 SURRENDERING TO THE VENGEFUL ITALIAN

Irresistible Mediterranean Tycoons

by Angela Bissell

Not even his foe's stunning daughter, Helena Shaw, will halt Leonardo Vincenti's vengeance. Leo knows that Helena would never willingly return to his side, so he blackmails her. But the passion that undid them before soon forces them *both* to the brink of surrender...

Natalia Di Sione hasn't left the family estate in years, but she must retrieve her grandfather's lost book of poems from Angelos Menas! The lives of the brooding Greek and his daughter were changed irrevocably by a fire, and Talia finds herself drawn to the formidable tycoon. She knows the untold pleasure Angelos offers is limited, but when she leaves with the book, will her heart remain on the island?

Read on for a sneak preview of
A DI SIONE FOR THE GREEK'S PLEASURE,
the sixth in the unmissable new eight book
Harlequin Presents® series
THE BILLIONAIRE'S LEGACY.

"Talia…" Angelos's voice broke on her name, and then, before she could even process what was happening, he pulled her toward him, his hands hard on her shoulders as his mouth crashed down on hers and plundered its soft depths.

It had been ten years since she'd been kissed, and then only a schoolboy's buss. She'd never been kissed like this, never felt every sense blaze to life, every nerve ending tingle with awareness, nearly painful in its intensity, as Angelos's mouth moved on hers and he pulled her tightly to him.

His hard contours collided against her softness, each point of contact creating an unbearably exquisite ache of longing as she tangled her hands in his hair and fit her mouth against his.

She was a clumsy, inexpert kisser, not sure what to do with her lips or tongue, only knowing that she wanted more of this. Of him.

She felt his hand slide down to cup her breast, his palm hot and hard through the thin material of her dress, and a gasp of surprise and delight escaped her.

That small sound of pleasure was enough to jolt Angelos out of his passion-fogged daze, for he dropped his hand and in one awful, abrupt movement tore his mouth from hers and stepped back.

"I'm sorry," he said, his voice coming out in a ragged gasp.

"No…" Talia pressed one shaky hand to her buzzing lips as she tried to blink the world back into focus. "Don't be sorry," she whispered. "It was wonderful."

"I shouldn't have—"

"Why not?" she challenged. She felt frantic with the desperate need to feel and taste him again, and more important, not to have him withdraw from her, not just physically, but emotionally. Angelos didn't answer and she forced herself to ask the question again. "Why not, Angelos?"

"Because you are my employee, and I was taking advantage of you," he gritted out. "It was not appropriate…"

"I don't care about appropriate," she cried. She knew she sounded desperate and even pathetic but she didn't care. She wanted him. She needed him. "I care about you," she confessed, her voice dropping to a choked whisper, and surprise and something worse flashed across Angelos's face. He shook his head, the movement almost violent and terribly final.

"No, Talia," he told her flatly. "You don't."

Don't miss
A DI SIONE FOR THE GREEK'S PLEASURE,
available December 2016 wherever
Harlequin Presents® books and ebooks are sold.

www.Harlequin.com

HARLEQUIN
Presents®

Christmas might be a time for giving, but in Lynne Graham's festive new duet Christmas with a Tycoon, *two Mediterranean billionaires are thinking only of what they can take!*

Italian tycoon Vito Zaffari is waiting out the festive season while a family scandal fades from the press. So he's come to his friend's snow-covered English country cottage, determined to shut out the world.

Until a beautiful bombshell dressed as Santa literally crashes into his Christmas! Innocent Holly Cleaver sneaks under Vito's defenses—he wants her like no other woman before and decides he *must* have her.

When Vito finds her gone the next day he's sure she'll be easy to forget…until he discovers that their one night of passion has a shocking Christmas consequence!

Don't miss

THE GREEK'S CHRISTMAS BRIDE

December 2016!

Stay Connected:

www.Harlequin.com

www.IHeartPresents.com

 /HarlequinBooks

 @HarlequinBooks

 /HarlequinBooks

HP13488